Red Clouds Dancing

THE SHADOWDANCE CLUB 6

AVERY GALE®

Chapter 1

Two months ago

CASH RED CLOUD looked around the small tavern and sighed. Recently, he'd begun to notice there were a lot of new people moving into the small town he'd always considered his home. Tonight, there were numerous people he didn't recognize in the small local bar, and he wasn't quite sure why the realization unsettled him—but it did.

It wasn't that he minded the little community's growth. In fact, he was all for it, but he'd always known every person in town, and it unnerved him to find himself suddenly surrounded by strangers. Perhaps it was time to start thinking about a new line of work, something that would keep him home more than he was gone.

He loved working as a black ops contractor for the Lamonts, but he was starting to feel as if it was time to give up his lifetime dream of finding a woman for him and his brothers to share. He'd always admired his parents' polyamorous relationship, but perhaps, it was time to look for something more traditional.

Taking another look around, he had to smile. He, along with his two brothers and sister, had always laughed about knowing everyone in town. Sure, there were times when it was a royal pain in the ass to have everyone up in your business, but it was also great to know there were a lot of people who had your back when life decided to send you skidding through a rough patch.

Each of his siblings had left Climax shortly after graduating from high school, and now it looked like they would all be moving home within a few months. He was heading to Houston first thing in the morning to help his two younger brothers get things together for their move home. He also needed to check on his youngest brother who was currently setting some kind of world record for the most *impatient* patient in Methodist Hospital's Neurological Institute.

Clay Red Cloud was the youngest of the Red Cloud sons and a champion bull rider in the Professional Bull Riders Association, or at least, he had been until he'd drawn Cyclone Charlie last weekend at an exhibition in his current hometown of Houston. Cash had watched the broadcast and had seen Clay take a nasty header into the fence. His concussion hadn't been particularly life-threatening. It had been one too many as far as the PBRA's docs were concerned, and they'd pulled his clearance for the foreseeable future.

Bringing his thoughts back to the moment, Cash glanced around again and wondered why no one had seen fit to build a nice place with a decent-sized dance floor. If the rumors he was hearing were true, this place would be closing soon, meaning all this business would leave their community.

He looked at his empty glass and smiled when the pretty blonde waitress asked him if he was ready for something stronger. Shaking his head, Cash figured the three glasses of tea he'd downed would be enough to keep him up most of the night, no reason to caffeinate any more of his brain cells. Hell, he might as well hit the road tonight because God knew he wasn't going to get any sleep, anyway.

Even though he didn't drink, he'd always loved going to dances. He loved any kind of dancing that involved holding a woman in his arms, always had. There was little Cash enjoyed more than the feeling of a woman's pillowy softness pressed against him as he moved her around a dance floor no larger than six steps from side to side.

For the past few months, Cash had been thinking about the old barn next to the large vacant lot he heard was earmarked as the site his bosses, Alex and Zach, had chosen for a new motel. He knew they had looked for a manager who would be a good fit in the free-thinking town of Climax. The Lamonts said they were willing to financially back the project but didn't want to operate it themselves.

Cash had heard them talking a few days ago about a woman Tori Bartell, Trace's new wife, had recommended. Since he'd noticed construction seemed to be starting, he had assumed that lead must have worked out. He knew his bosses wouldn't have started the project if they didn't have someone hired because they were devoted to their family and already busy with various businesses. Laughing to himself, he remembered hearing them say more than once their toddler triplets were easier to manage than their wife, and everyone who knew Katarina Lamont understood.

Sliding off his stool, he decided to head home to throw a few things in a bag before heading south. The middle Red Cloud brother, Collin had been looking out for Clay and was probably ready to kill him by now. The two younger Red Cloud brothers barely managed to tolerate each other enough to share a home—Collin had been able to buy something large enough they rarely crossed paths.

Collin had just turned thirty, decided he missed mountain living, and was heading back to Climax. Cash shook his head in wonder at his younger brother. The damned kid had more money than anybody needed. Collin had decided computer programming was a lot more interesting than college and dropped out his junior year to write games. Cash had been convinced his parents were going to come apart at the seams, but it didn't take long for everyone to be convinced the middle Red Cloud son had known exactly what he was doing.

Collin had become a millionaire by the time he was twenty-five, and Cash shuddered to think what he was worth now. But despite his fortune and the fact Collin was what Cash considered almost scary smart, he also tended to be something of a loner.

Cash wasn't sure the kid had ever even been on a real date after leaving college. Collin had been staying at the hospital with Clay, but during their last phone call, Cash knew it was just a matter of time before Collin tossed his younger brother out of the nearest—and probably highest—window.

Then a couple of weeks ago, Cash had talked to Alex and Zach who agreed turning the barn into a bar and dance club would be a great added attraction for Climax and offered to help Cash in any way they could, including giving him a lifetime lease on the property for a dollar a year. They'd toured the old barn and saw it could be easily be revamped.

Red Clouds Dancing would be a great name for the place. He smiled at the thought. His ancestors had been warriors with a strong history of dance, honoring nature and clouds play, predominantly in Navajo legends. Cash had always been immensely proud of his heritage, so honoring it in the name of his new endeavor seemed only fitting.

LAYLA LANG WAS certain supervising the building of a motel that was supposed to look like a cross between a medieval castle and a chalet was going to be a labor of *tortured love*, but she planned to throw herself into the task. When her friend, Tori called her a couple weeks ago, she had been thrilled at the prospect of a job in her chosen field. The chance at a job that would allow her to be in on the project from the very beginning was a dream come true.

The video interview she'd had a few days later had been short and sweet. Basically, Alex and Zach Lamont had outlined their vision, asked her if she would be interested, then thrown out numbers for a salary and benefits package, including stock shares. She'd been shocked at their generosity and told them so. When they had turned to each other and started discussing temporary housing options for her, she'd interrupted and asked if she had the job.

Zach had chuckled and asked, "Layla, did Tori tell you anything about us? Did she mention that we're, well—determined, forthright, pushy—"

"Dominant," Alex had finished for him.

"Well, not really, no. She mentioned this motel would be loosely connected with the ShadowDance Club, but she said I needed to meet you and form my own opinion. And, well... she might have mentioned that I'd have to have my head up my ass to pass up this opportunity." Layla smiled and shook her head at the memory of their conversation.

Tori Paulson, now Tori Bartell, *had* mentioned her

husband was a Dom, but her sweet friend had sworn she'd never been happier, and considering Tori's history of abuse at the hands of a stalker, that was saying a lot. When Tori had mentioned The Club in the same conversation, Layla had wondered what a dance club had to do with Tori's sex life, but she wasn't about to mention that to the two men filling her computer monitor that's for sure.

Layla had planned to research the Lamonts and the community of Climax, but she'd been so overwhelmed with finals and graduation paperwork, she simply hadn't had the time.

"I'm going to cut to the chase, Layla." Alex Lamont's voice startled her back to the moment. "The job was yours the minute Tori Bartell recommended you. We like Tori and have a great deal of respect for her professional opinion as well."

She watched as he nodded to his brother, then Zach addressed her.

"Layla, we'd like you to move to Climax at your earliest convenience. We'll send you expense money for moving. Should you get here and not like it for some reason, we'll pay your expenses to move again." He laughed, and she was sure it was because she was gaping at him. "Don't look so surprised, I just promised you something I know I'm not going to have to deliver because I'm sure you're going to fit in perfectly and love our small community."

Zach's words had made her laugh, and they got right back to the business end of their discussion. She liked that they weren't pushovers by any means, but she sincerely appreciated how they'd both listened intently and made suggestions for making her move easier—including vetoing her idea do it all herself to save them money.

The Lamonts had smoothly maneuvered her until they'd won every point of the discussion, and each one had been to her benefit. It was almost as if she'd gained a couple of "Big Brothers" rather than bosses by the time they'd ended the conversation.

Layla couldn't remember a time she'd been so excited, she could barely sit still. She'd called Tori immediately to tell her she'd be seeing her in a couple of weeks, and her friend had laughed at the way she was practically bouncing in her seat. Tori had been wonderful to work with at the law firm despite everything she'd been going through at the time.

Most of the attorneys and their administrative staff had treated Layla like she was about a half a step above pond scum, but Tori had always been pleasant and friendly. She was the only one of the attorneys who had never seemed to even notice the disparity in their positions. When Layla had told Tori about her interview, she'd been every bit as excited as Layla. Then her sweet friend had assured her she would indeed love Climax and her wonderful, though slightly insane, new friends.

Now it was only three days until graduation, and Layla was putting the last of her measly personal belongings in a small box since this was her last day at the law office. Sure, having everything packed three hours before she could make her escape might be a little pathetic, but she didn't care. Layla could hardly wait to walk out the door for the last time. Just as she folded the box closed, she noticed a huge black pickup pull up in front of the building's floor-to-ceiling front windows. It wasn't that pickups were anything unusual in Texas, but they weren't all that often found parked in front of prestigious law firms in downtown Houston at two in the afternoon either.

Layla found her attention diverted to the gorgeous cowboy walking around the truck's front end and through the front doors. He was amazingly tall, and his hair gleamed black in the bright May sunshine. His aviator glasses and broad shoulders gave him an air of barely leashed danger. As if he'd heard her mental assessment, he seemed to zero in on her with radar-like accuracy.

By the time he was standing directly in front of the large reception desk where she was working, every nerve ending in her body felt like it had been electrified.

"Hello, my name is Cash Red Cloud. Are you Layla Lang?" The man's voice was like rich dark chocolate, smooth as silk and probably not safe in large quantities. Despite his height, he was well-muscled, and his Native American heritage was easy to see. His skin was the color of sweet caramel, and his short hair so black, it glistened under the lobby's bright lights. Suddenly, she realized he was smiling at her and patiently waiting for her reply to his question.

"Oh, yes, I'm Layla. Can I help you?" She'd been surprised when he'd known her name, hell, half the firm's employees probably couldn't tell you her full name.

"Is that yours?" he asked, nodding toward the small box she'd just finished filling.

"Well, yes, as a matter of fact, it is. I just finished packing up my desk. Today is my last day here." She'd answered him but was sure he'd be able to hear the questions in her tone.

"So, I've been told." He smiled at her, and she could tell he was enjoying her confusion. "I'm sorry, sweetheart, I shouldn't be messing with you, but you are absolutely gorgeous with that befuddled expression. We have some mutual friends, Alex and Zach Lamont. When they found out I was going to be in town to help my brothers pack, they asked me to pick you up and deliver you to a very special place where their wife, Katarina, and your friend, Tori are sending you to as a gift. So… since I have no desire to be on Kat's bad side and I also know better than to piss off the local attorney, let's get you loaded up and off to your fun afternoon."

"But I don't get off work until five o'clock. I can't just leave early. I'll get in trouble." Even as the words were crossing her lips, she knew how absurd they sounded. Hell, it wasn't as if they could fire her or anything, but still, she had never been one to shirk on her duties. She didn't want that shadow following her, no matter how far she was going to be from "Prick, Dick, and Ass-ociates Law Firm."

Pulling out his phone, she watched as he typed in a short message, then smiled at her. Almost immediately, the desk phone rang. She answered and listened as Mrs. Rich in Human Resources told her she was free to leave at any time, actually thanked her for her dedication and assured her she'd be paid for the entire day. The woman—who had never even actually spoken to her in the two years she'd worked there—also promised they would be forwarding digital copies of various letters of recommendation to her new e-mail account. *I have a new e-mail account?*

All the time she'd been on the phone, Mr. Hottie Cowboy had stood in front of her, watching her. His gaze was so intent, she wondered if he would be able to see directly into her soul if she'd returned his look long enough.

Layla had no sooner hung up the desk phone than her cell phone rang. She smiled when she saw Tori's number on the display. When she answered, she heard her friend's soft laughter.

"Hey there, sweet friend… got a hot-looking fella

standing in front of ya? Isn't he yummy?" Layla could tell Tori had turned to someone else when she said, "Hey! I didn't mean yummy for me... I meant yummy for my single pal. I've already got all the yummy I can handle."

When Tori giggled, then redirected her conversation to her, Layla shook her head.

"Sorry, my sweet husband is a bit possessive. Now, is Cash there?" Layla knew her face was flaming a brilliant red because there was no doubt the man in front of her had heard her friend's questions. His grin was a dead giveaway.

"Yes, as a matter of fact, he is. Don't suppose you'd be interested in enlightening me, would you?" She knew her words didn't hold any real bite. Hell's bells, the only thing she wanted to bite was standing in front of her, watching her with an intensity that might have intimidated a lesser woman. But she was determined to stand tall and at least appear unaffected.

"Cash is a good friend, and when Kat and I found out he was going to be in Houston... well, we did some *planning* and enlisted our men's help." Tori giggled, but then her tone turned serious. "You know I'd never send someone you couldn't trust, right? Well, anyway, we wanted to do something special for you for your graduation. Oh, girlfriend, this is your lucky day. Please just go along with Cash. He has very specific instructions." Tori's bubbling laughter was infectious, and Layla couldn't help but smile. "Oh, and you getting off early is compliments of Zach Lamont's charm. Go and enjoy. I'll see you soon." Tori disconnected before Layla's thoughts caught up enough to respond.

Staring at her phone in stunned disbelief, Layla was finally jarred back to the present by Cash's soft laughter.

"She's something else. Hell, they all are—you'll see

that soon enough. Now, let's get a move on before we're late to your appointment and I'm in hot water with my friends." He picked up the small box she'd packed and escorted her out of the building.

When she got closer to the large truck, she hesitated, wondering how she was going to get into it without a stepladder. *Damned pencil skirt, anyway.* She'd been riding the bus since selling her small car a few weeks ago. Honestly, it had been on its last legs and probably wouldn't have made it to Colorado, anyway, but she'd still been sad about letting it go.

Cash moved first to the truck's rear door, placing her small box on the back seat before opening the passenger door. He simply leaned over and effortlessly scooped her up into his arms. She let out a startled breath as he settled her onto the seat as if she didn't weigh anything at all. He smiled at her gasp of surprise while leaning across and securing her seat belt. After he'd snapped the two ends together, he kissed her on the forehead.

"You smell good enough to eat, sweetheart—like fresh strawberries." His double meaning wasn't lost on her, and she felt her face flush again. He was chuckling again as he closed her door.

Chapter 2

Present day

C ASH LEANED BACK and watched as the last of the liquor was placed on the glass shelves behind the bar as the bartenders quickly finished up last-minute details for tonight's Grand Opening. Cash had been pleasantly surprised at how quickly they'd been able to get the place up and running.

It had turned out that Clay Red Cloud was something of a marvel as a designer and renovator. He and Collin had teased their youngest brother that he'd done a great job with the place because he'd been in every bar west of the Mississippi during his PBRA days.

Collin had moved back to Climax at the same time, and his renovations to their parents' rambling ranch home had turned the place into a technological dream space. They'd spent weeks asking everyone who knew Layla Lang questions about her preferences and tastes in everything from colors to furnishings. The entire house had been decorated with her in mind. They'd built a suite of rooms at the end of the hall leading to a wing they'd added as a special gift for the blonde bombshell motel manager the Lamonts had hired.

When he'd gone to help his brothers move home a

couple of months ago, he hadn't hesitated when his bosses had asked him to escort their newly hired motel manager to an appointment. Hell, he'd have done almost anything to get out of that damned hospital—his brother Clay had to be the worst patient on the planet.

Clay had been damned lucky the header he'd taken during his last PBRA performance hadn't snapped his fool neck. Every time Cash watched the films, he marveled at how Clay had come through with nothing but a moderately severe concussion. Not that he and Collin hadn't considered wringing his fool neck themselves a time or two during Clay's last hospital stay, but the damned kid had been asking for it if you asked Cash.

Even though he understood Clay's worry about an uncertain future, he hadn't been inclined to tolerate his younger sibling's habit of growling at anyone who wanted to discuss other options with him. Christ, talk about vying for the title King of Denial. Cash had wanted to polish his crown and hand the Prince of Pissy a scepter and sing that damned coronation song they played at graduations.

All things considered, it hadn't been any hardship to walk out and leave Collin to deal with Clay for a few hours so he could help Katarina Lamont and Victoria Bartell do something nice for Climax's soon-to-be-newest-citizen.

Kat and Tori were both sweethearts, and when they'd sworn that he'd be happy he'd helped them, Cash had assumed he'd probably get some kind of sappy gift from them. Even now, he laughed to himself when he thought back on how he'd hoped their gift wouldn't be something they'd cooked themselves. Damn, their reputations as being culinary disasters were nearly legendary.

The minute he'd walked into the lobby of the law firm where Tori had worked before moving to Climax, Cash had known exactly what the two had meant about being grateful. The woman sitting at the reception desk had stolen his breath.

Despite his reputation as the one who always kept his cool when everything around him was going from sunshine to shit, he'd been completely thunderstruck by Layla. Her hourglass figure had curves in all the right places, and she had the face of an angel. He'd never cared a thing for stick-thin women—what man wanted someone they had to worry they'd break into pieces the first time he fucked her against the wall?

Layla's skin was the clearest shade of ivory he'd ever seen, and Cash bet it turned to the color of perfect pearls under the full moon. Years ago, his Navajo grandmother had told him to "watch for the woman who shines in the moonlight," and he'd always assumed her words were figurative. Now, after meeting Layla, he wasn't so sure.

Cash loved all three of his fathers, but he hadn't ever been convinced he and his two brothers would be able to successfully replicate their success sharing a wife. The elder Red Cloud brothers were all as different as he and his brothers, but somehow, they'd always seemed to use their strengths and weaknesses in a strange, well-choreographed dance that, oddly enough, always seemed to work out to everyone's benefit.

The one thing that had never been in question was the three elder Red Cloud siblings' total devotion to their mother. The problem was he and his brothers had always had vastly different tastes in women. Sighing, Cash thought back and honestly couldn't ever remember a time when any of them had ever even been remotely attracted to the same woman.

As he'd walked across the lobby the day they met, he'd

heard Layla talking to herself—it had sounded like a mental list of things she needed to get done before Sunday, and it had sounded like a pretty long list. As he'd approached the desk, she'd focused on him, and he could have sworn she was undressing him with her eyes. It had taken his considerable control to keep his unruly cock under control.

Later, as he'd maneuvered them through the thick traffic, he finally broke the silence in the truck. "It sounded like you have a pretty significant list of things to do before Sunday." At her surprised look, he added, "You were talking to yourself, beautiful." When he smiled, she finally seemed to relax. "Now… what's happening on Sunday?" He'd been pleasantly surprised by her brilliant smile as she explained.

"Oh… my graduation. I have a lot to do so I may have to miss it. And… well… damn it, I'd been looking forward to it, you know? I've worked really hard to get to this point and well… hell's bells, I guess it doesn't really matter. I don't have anyone coming anyway, so…"

She didn't finish the sentence, but he'd seen the pain in her eyes before she'd turned and stared out of her window. Cash had already figured out it was damned important to her as it should be, but when he heard her sniff back tears, his heart had nearly broken for her.

He didn't want to embarrass her by drawing attention to her disappointment or her tears, so he just continued with his end of the conversation. When he offered to help her with her list and to enlist the help of his brothers if need be, she was thrilled. He delivered her to the address he'd been given and watched her eyes widen in shock.

According to Kat and Tori, The Bonita Spa was a luxury day spa—*what the fuck ever that was*—that would be providing Layla with an afternoon of pure decadent pampering. The place was a black granite wonder, at least from the outside. When he turned to look at his passenger, she was gaping at him open-mouthed.

Cash had grinned at her as he explained, "Beautiful, this is a gift from your girlfriends in Climax. They wanted you to be 'pampered and properly primed'—their words, not mine, by the way—before your big day. So, you see, it's important for you to attend your graduation." He watched as her pretty emerald eyes filled with tears before the big drops finally breaching her lower lids and spilled over. He reached over and wiped them away with his thumbs before he pulled her closer. "Don't cry, love. Mercy, Kat and Tori will skin me alive if I take you in there looking like someone kicked your new puppy." He gave her a quick hug when she smiled.

"Come on, beautiful, let's get you inside before you're late." After he'd left her in the capable hands of the spa staff and double-checked the other gifts her friends had sent had arrived, he told her to be sure and wait inside the spa when she was finished, and he'd come back for her. He planned to be back with plenty of time to spare, but years of Special Forces training was never far from the surface, and backup plans were his second nature.

After making several phone calls, he made his way back to the medical center to check on Clay. When he saw his brother's room was filled with family and friends, he pulled Collin off to the side. Collin had always been the family "Brainiac" and certainly had the accolades and bank balance to prove it, so when Cash had inquired about Collin's plans for dinner that night, his younger brother's skepticism hadn't been a surprise.

Grinning Cash just said, "Let's go, I'll tell you on the way." Then he leaned close to Clay and spoke low enough no one else could hear. "I'll call you later, gotta run. Don't make any plans for your last day in Houston. I'll explain later." He wanted to preempt any chance Clay wouldn't be able to attend Layla's graduation. Not only did Cash want Layla to have friends there because it was obviously a worthy accomplishment, he also wanted his brothers to meet her. Their grandmother had always sworn they would follow their family's long history of polyamorous marriage, and for the first time, Cash had sensed his grandmother's prediction might be fulfilled.

Cash remembered how Collin had been more than a little skeptical when he'd insisted he needed to meet Layla, or at least, he had been until she walked into the waiting room at the spa. Collin told him later, he'd felt like the floor had completely fallen away from beneath his feet and had known in that instant that she was their *One*.

At Cash's subtle, unspoken signal, Collin had stood back and watched while he greeted Layla because Cash had seen her eyes darting hesitatingly between them when she'd walked into the luxurious lobby. They'd laughed later about the large bag she'd been carrying and how she'd seemed reluctant to hand it over. When Kat and Tori explained later it had been full of racy lingerie, they'd understood why she'd been so protective of its secrets.

When he'd introduced her to Collin, his brother had stepped forward and grasped both of her small hands in his.

"I'm so pleased to meet you, Layla. You are everything Cash said you were and more." Collin had smiled when her pretty green eyes went wide, then dropped to the floor. They'd both immediately recognized Layla as a submissive, but neither of them believed she was going to be easy to convince. He remembered watching as she seemed to gather her defenses around her like a cloak and had instinctively known patience was the only way to win her heart.

Cash had been sure the next few days would be a flurry of activity, but he'd suddenly felt energized by the prospect. Walking her back to his truck from the spa, they'd made sure one of them was touching her at all times and noticed she had seemed disconcerted by how much she liked it. Obviously, she'd been on her own for a long time in a large city, so she wasn't accustomed to being taken care of. He'd been determined at that moment to move heaven and earth to make her theirs.

As they pulled out into traffic, she'd graciously thanked them for giving her a ride back to the office so she could catch the bus. He'd been caught off guard by her assumption he would just leave her off at a bus stop when it would be dark in a few minutes. She'd casually mentioned how grateful she was she wouldn't have to walk all the way home from the spa since it was quite a hike, and her neighborhood wasn't a place any sane person wanted to stroll through after dark.

Cash knew the look he and Collin had given her must have been mirror images of incredulous disbelief because she'd looked between them and immediately stopped chattering. They'd both said *"No"* at the same time, and the vehemence in their responses had startled her. They'd been stopped at a red light, so he'd been able to watch her closely as she'd launched into a frustrated tirade.

"What the holy heck? No, what? No, you won't give me a ride back to the office? Or... well, I guess I don't even really know what else you might be barking *no* about. So, well, I guess if you'll just drop me at the next bus stop, I'll figure it out, and you'll be off the hook." She hadn't been able to keep the disappointment and hurt out of her voice even though he knew she tried.

He knew his voice had been more growl than it should have been, but at the time, he'd been very close to pulling her over his knee and paddling her very fine ass.

"No to the bus, period."

Most women would have had the good sense to stop rattling on, but not Layla. She just went right on with her ridiculous rambling.

"Well, alrighty then. But I'm going on record as not appreciating having to walk all that way in these 'fuck me' shoes Tori sent me. Did you know they took my other clothes and wouldn't give them back? Damn, that frosted my cookies. I liked that skirt, hell, it was the best thing I'd ever found at Goodwill... but never mind that now. These shoes,"—pointing to the heels she was now wearing—"are going to make me stand out like a sore thumb in my neck of the woods, I tell ya. Hell, these shoes probably cost more than some of my neighbors make in a month of Sundays. Well... the ones who have legitimate jobs, anyway."

She took a deep breath and let out a frustrated sigh, trying valiantly to hide her disappointment, but both he and Collin could see the stress of everything was finally catching up with her.

Chapter 3

C ASH SHOOK HIS head and laughed as he remembered how he'd recently surprised Layla by reminding her about how quickly he maneuvered to the right-hand lane and exited the highway that first evening in Houston. When he'd told her how close she'd come to getting her sweet ass warmed up that night, she'd turned a beautiful shade of crimson. The two of them had been talking as they'd eaten the small picnic lunch he'd packed as a surprise for her and had laughed at the memory of their first misunderstanding.

When they'd all first moved back to Climax, each of them had been completely swamped with work obligations. They'd only seen each other in passing and for an occasional get-together with friends, but Cash had never doubted he and his brothers would go after her as soon as the timing was right.

Cash, Collin, and Clay had been working nearly day and night to get the renovations to their home and the dance club completed on ridiculously ambitious timetables. Now, with all the updates to their home wrapped up and the construction on the bar and grill complete, he, Collin, and Clay had begun what they'd affectionately dubbed "Project Layla."

That first afternoon, when he'd kidnapped her for two

hours during the day, he'd packed a small picnic lunch. Cash had led her down to the creek behind the motel, and they'd dangled their feet in the crystal-clear water and talked as they'd eaten the sandwiches and raw vegetables he knew she loved to snack on. She'd been overjoyed when she'd seen the fresh strawberries and white cake without frosting. He'd laughed out loud at her squeal of delight when he'd pulled a small container of Cool Whip from the little ice chest. But he'd shaken his head and disagreed when she'd compared the treat to good sex.

"Layla, I remember our last night in the condo before we left Houston, and I'm absolutely positive these strawberries don't compare to the pleasure we all felt that night."

They'd both been quiet for long minutes, lost in the memories of lust-fueled passion of that night. He'd finally broken the silence by asking her if she planned to attend Red Clouds Dancing's Grand Opening. When she'd assured him she would be there with bells on, he'd spontaneously pulled her into his embrace. She'd gone completely still before she'd finally relaxed, and he'd almost groaned out loud when he felt her nipples peak beneath her thin cotton shirt as he held her tightly against his chest.

After he'd taken her back to work, Cash had returned to the club. Sitting down in the main bar area with a stack of invoices he needed to review, he'd quickly found himself staring at his work but not seeing anything on the paper in his hands, letting his memories lead him back to that first night in Houston before he and Collin had taken Layla to her apartment.

"When did you last eat a full meal, Layla?" He knew by the look on her face he wasn't going to like the answer.

When she'd stammered, "Well, I'm guessing the bologna sandwich I had for lunch today doesn't count as a full meal, right?" he'd simply raised an eyebrow in question, so she continued, "Yeah, that's what I figured. Well, in that case...hmmm, let's see."

Cash hadn't given her any more time to answer, he'd simply pulled in and parked at the next decent restaurant he'd seen. He'd opened his door and pulled her over so he could help her step down out of the truck.

"We'll be having a discussion about taking proper care of yourself later, love."

Hell, it appeared taking proper care of herself was going to be an ongoing lesson with Layla. He and his brothers had all reminded her of the importance of that lesson more times than he cared to remember during the past two months. The blasted woman still continued skipping so many meals, she'd lost entirely too much weight. During a recent conversation with Tori, he'd also learned she'd had a nasty bout of flu, something she had yet to mention to any of them.

Thinking back on their dinner that first night, he remembered how tense things had been, but even then Cash had known he was mostly to blame. He'd been so frustrated that she thought they'd allow her to traipse around a seedy neighborhood, looking like she'd just stepped out of some fashion magazine—and that wasn't even taking in to account she was hungry. Hell, he'd barely spoken a word to her during their meal. As they'd finished dessert, he turned to her and tried to school his expression.

"Layla, I want to make something perfectly clear. We were *not* trying to get rid of you nor did we have any intention of letting you ride a city bus at night. Hell, just thinking about you riding on one of those things scares the hell out of me."

The drive to Layla's small apartment hadn't taken long. When they parked in front of her building, Cash saw Collin's eyes darken as he took in their surroundings. Layla waved off their concerned looks, assuring them it was a typical Friday night in her neighborhood. Hell, even now, he shuddered every time he remembered the events of that evening.

Once they'd made their way inside her tiny apartment, Cash looked around and known she was nearly finished packing for her move to Colorado. Cash stood back as Collin looked around.

"How long will it take you to finish packing if we help?" Collin asked the question as he started moving a box closer to the door.

She shrugged her shoulders, then finally admitted it would probably only take an hour or so. When she asked why they wanted to know, neither Cash nor Collin answered, they'd simply told her to get to work.

He and Collin started moving things to the door, and after Layla moved down the short hallway into what Cash had assumed was her bedroom, he looked at Collin in silent question. Collin had been much too quiet, and Cash was betting his wealthy brother hadn't been in a neighborhood like Layla's in years. Cash almost laughed out loud when Collin finally regained enough composure to start swearing under his breath.

"I can't fucking believe our woman lived in this place— a ground-floor apartment in this part of the city? Christ, it's a miracle she survived long enough for you to find her."

The words had barely left his lips when they heard a gunshot from the apartment above. He and Collin had both taken off toward the small room Layla had disappeared into. She looked up, startled by their sudden appearance, but oddly enough, hadn't uttered a sound when the gun had fired above her.

"What?" When they had both stared at her in disbelief, she seemed to catch on. "Oh, that?" pointing to the ceiling. "Never mind that, he used to do it a lot, but I made it clear he can't shoot at the floor anymore, so it's not a big problem now." While they stood dumbfounded, she turned back to the small bag she was filling as if her words were perfectly reasonable.

Collin dropped his face in his hands and shook his head back and forth. "Un-fucking-believable. 'He can't shoot at the floor *anymore*'? Are you serious? Christ, almighty. I'll be in the living room." Collin turned to Cash. "She's all yours, big brother. I was going to stop you if you started with her tonight, but not now."

Cash would have laughed at the absurdity of the situation if he hadn't been so utterly astonished by the whole thing. Collin stormed from the room, leaving Cash with Layla who was watching them with a baffled expression that quickly transformed into a wall of defense when she met Cash's eyes. He knew it was a look she was accustomed to calling on.

Taking a deep breath, Cash knew it was time to choose his battles carefully. Cash decided he needed to pull together every bit of tact he could manage if they were going to get her out of there that night, so he smiled and purposely softened his tone.

"Love, we are more than a little concerned for your safety. Let's get your things together and move them tonight."

Just as she opened her mouth to protest, he heard a loud knocking on the front door. She tried to push past him, calling out, "Don't answer that, Collin, please. If you do—" but her words were too late, Collin had already pulled the door open, and a very drunk man stood in the doorway, wearing boxer shorts, sandals, and nothing else.

"Hey, who are you and where is the hot chick who lives here? There's never anybody else here. Oh, there you are, chicka, how's about a date?" The man's words had been slurred, and his gaze locked onto her chest.

"Jimmy, go back to your wife, you know you aren't supposed to be here. Don't make me call her." Layla had stepped forward and shaken her finger in the drunk's face before closing the door with him still standing there, then turned to Collin.

"Now, don't open that door again, you hear me, mister? This happens sometimes, and it may happen again before you and Cash get out of here, so just… well, just… don't." She'd turned on her heel and flounced herself right back into her bedroom.

Cash had watched her walk away and turned to his brother. "I can't fucking believe this shit. How on earth has she done this? How could anyone manage to study in this insane place? Hell, she must have an I.Q. to rival yours. Tori told me she has a 4.0 average. How could she do that living in this loony bin?"

That had probably been the second time in their entire lives Cash had actually seen Collin speechless. Hell, the guy had started talking in full sentences at eighteen months and had rarely come up for air since. There had been a small part of Cash that wanted to whip out his phone and video the whole scene because he was sure neither his parents nor Clay would ever believe it—and they hadn't.

Finally, Collin's jaw had snapped closed, and Cash would have sworn you could hear his brain come back online. "I have no words—honest to God—there are no words that would tell you what I'm thinking." With that, Collin had shaken his head as he'd turned and walked back to begin once again moving boxes closer to the door.

There had been two more incidents with knocking at the door before they'd managed to get all of Layla's belongings loaded into his truck. It had taken a long time to load because he'd insisted Collin stand guard, so nothing was stolen while he moved the boxes. They'd left Layla cooling her heels inside the truck's air-conditioned cab.

She hadn't been pleased by what she termed their "steam-rolling tactics," and he'd assured her she hadn't begun to see "steam-rolled" yet. He'd known she must have called Tori to complain about how things were working out because he'd gotten a text from Alex Lamont that had simply read: *Do what you need to do to keep her safe.*

They'd quickly settled Layla in the larger of the available guest rooms despite her protests she should be in a motel. After she'd settled in, they'd sat around the kitchen island, talking and enjoying a nice cold beer. When he'd seen her eyelids beginning to droop, he'd smiled.

"Love, why don't you go take a shower and hit the hay. I can see those dark circles under your eyes, so I know you must be dead on your feet. Collin and I will check in with you before we go to bed ourselves to see if you need anything."

It had been like watching a movie as the beautiful woman sitting between them had just stared blankly ahead. He and Collin sat transfixed as her eyelids fluttered and finally slid closed. She hadn't made any effort to move, and when he had reached over to cradle the side of her pale face in his palm, she hadn't even stirred at his touch. When her fingers had gone lax around the bottle she'd been holding, he'd wondered if she was going to melt into a puddle at their feet. Cash had looked up at Collin, and his brother just smiled and shaken his head.

"Unbelievable. She is utterly exhausted. Can you imagine trying to get any real rest in that hell hole she was living in? Come on, I'll help you with her shower, then we can get her into bed. I know she'll sleep better if we get the stench of that place off her. How she managed to keep her little part of hell so clean is a miracle in itself. Did you look around? Hell, you could have eaten off the fucking floors."

She had barely stirred when Cash picked her up in his arms and carried her down the hall. By the time Cash had gotten her undressed, Collin had warmed up the large walk-in shower and stood in his boxers, waiting to take her into the large enclosure.

While Cash had been stripping down to his briefs, he heard Collin speaking to her in soft tones and her sleepy replies. Once they'd gotten her cleaned up and dry, they tucked her into the king-sized bed. They'd left a small dresser lamp on so she wouldn't be frightened waking up in a strange place during the night. Leaving her sleeping peacefully, they'd found their way to their own rooms.

Cash smiled thinking back on how anxious he'd been for her to meet Clay. He'd known Collin had been texting Clay about her earlier and had seen him take her picture when she hadn't been watching. Cash knew Collin had sent the photo to their younger brother.

He'd been ready to slide into bed but hadn't been able to resist the temptation to check in on her one last time. After waiting his entire life for her, it had been pure torture knowing she was just down the hall sleeping peacefully. As he had started to slip into her room, he'd heard Collin step out of his room into the hall.

"You, too?" They had both chuckled at their like-minded thinking.

"Yeah, I just wanted to see her one last time before I went to sleep." As they walked quietly on bare feet until they were close to the bed, Collin had looked at him and smiled. "She is amazing. Honestly, I had started to think we were never going to find her." Cash looked on as Collin reached forward and straightened the light blanket, then softly trailed the back of one finger over her cheek to move aside a stray curl.

"She's perfect. Well, maybe she'll need some guidance on taking better care of herself, but really, she is simply breathtaking. Our little brother is faunching at the bit to meet her, too. I promised him we'd bring her when we pick him up tomorrow."

Cash had simply nodded, leaned forward, and kissed her lightly on the forehead before he'd muttered, "Let's get out of here before we wake her, and she thinks we're a couple of crazed stalkers."

Chapter 4

C ASH HAD BEEN so deeply submerged in the memories, he hadn't noticed when Clay came in and sat down next to him until he heard his youngest brother laugh.

"Damn, brother, where were you? I can't even imagine what it takes to distract a former SEAL enough, he doesn't know someone has approached him, let alone sat down on the next bar stool."

"No shit. I was just remembering Layla in Houston and how much has happened in the past two months." He sighed and looked around the empty room. In a couple of hours, they'd be swamped, but for now, the place was pretty quiet. "How did your time with Layla go yesterday? I haven't had a chance to check in with you."

Clay grinned like the fun-loving guy he'd been before his accident. Cash was glad his brother was finally finding out there really was life off the rodeo circuit.

"It was great. I took her out to the Bartells', and Trace let us ride a couple of their horses. We didn't ride far because I didn't want Layla to get saddle sore, well, at least not from a fucking horse. Anyway, she really seemed to enjoy it. It was good to see her smile. She's been so damned busy with that motel and doesn't take any time off that I can tell. Did you know she'd been sick?" At Cash's nod, Clay added, "Tori mentioned it to me briefly, but she didn't want me to tell Layla she'd blabbed."

Cash knew Clay was right about Layla not taking enough time off. It was one thing they all had in common—their work ethics kept them too busy to enjoy life. But that was coming to a screeching halt if Cash had anything to say about it.

Alex and Zach Lamont had come in yesterday and had lunch with him. Cash hadn't been so naive he hadn't known his friends had something on their minds, so he'd finally just told them to spit it out. Of course, it was Alex who had met his challenge head-on.

"Cash, we're worried you and your brothers are making a mistake with Layla. She is working too hard, and from things she said to Rissa and Katarina recently at the spa, she's decided you guys are no longer interested in her as anything other than a friend, so she's planning to apply for a membership at ShadowDance."

The ShadowDance Club was the Lamont brothers' very exclusive and extremely successful BDSM club. Cash hadn't been able to decide what shocked him more, the fact she thought they were no longer interested in her or that she'd even consider applying for a membership to The Club.

"Has she submitted an application yet?" Cash had barely been able to spit out the question.

This time it was Zach who answered, "No, but honestly if she does, we won't have any legitimate reason to reject it. Sure, we can stall a few days, but we all know she'll sail through the clearance process. We'd already done all her background checks when Tori first suggested her for the manager position at the motel."

Collin had pulled up a chair and asked what they were talking about. When Cash answered, Col had nearly spit out his beer.

"Are you fucking kidding me? Why on earth would she apply to The Club?" Cash had watched his brother's expression change from confusion to fury as Zach had explained what Mitch had picked up on the monitors the day before.

Cash and both of his brothers agreed they owed the Lamonts a large debt of thanks for the heads-up, then they sat down to discuss the best way to kick "Project Layla" into a higher gear—a *much* higher gear.

LAYLA DIDN'T UNDERSTAND why she was so nervous about attending the Grand Opening at Red Clouds Dancing this evening, but she'd gone through her entire closet like a Tasmanian devil, leaving her small bedroom looking like an F-5 tornado had passed through. She finally settled on a short denim skirt and topped it with a fitted white T-shirt. Adding a bright red bandana and her red cowboy boots made the outfit perfect.

She was happy with the way her clothes were fitting now that she'd dropped a few pounds, but she knew the Red Cloud brothers hadn't seemed as impressed with her weight loss. *Just another clue they've lost interest, Layla. Time to get a clue, girl!*

She spent over an hour in the bathtub, thinking back to the night in Houston when all three brothers had made love to her, and she was now running late, but damn that was some night. Even if all she ever had was the sweet memory, it had been so worth it.

Every time she let her mind wander back to that night,

it was as if she could feel the way her entire body had hummed with awareness as Cash and Clay had led her down the hall in the condo. And when they'd reached the bedroom she'd been using, they both peeled off their shirts, and since they'd already been barefoot, that had left them clad in faded Wranglers that did nothing to hide their obvious arousal.

The two of them worked quickly to free her from the yoga pants and short tank top she was using as pajamas, then laid her out on the bed. She could still remember how the goosebumps felt racing over her skin as they'd stood beside the bed admiring her like she was some kind of prize.

When they finally climbed onto the enormous bed and flanked her, she nearly moaned aloud at their first touch. She could still feel their fingers tracing the curves of her breasts, then following unseen lines over her hips until they each grasped a thigh and pulled her legs wide apart. The first brush of the cool air in the room ignited every nerve ending in her already throbbing pussy, and she wasn't able to suppress her gasp. Layla hadn't even realized she'd closed her eyes until she heard Collin's voice from the doorway.

"Are you two going to just play, or are you going to give her the relief she seeks?"

She watched Clay smile up from where he'd been worshipping her tightly budded pink nipples. It hadn't taken her long to figure out Clay was a breast man... he told her he loved breasts because they were the givers of life, and for most women, they were extremely sensitive.

Layla hadn't even tried to hold back her smile when he told her that hers were perfect because they would pillow a child in need of comfort, and they'd also be perfect for fucking… then waggled his eyebrows up and down in true comic fashion. She mentally shook her head at his antics, but she truly loved his sense of the absurd as much as she loved Cash's strength and Collin's dominance.

"Oh, she's going to get to come, I promise you that," Clay grinned. "Hell, she's going to come until she doesn't think she can possibly do it again, then we'll wring one or two more from this sweet body."

Looking in the mirror now, Layla remembered how her entire body heated from the fire igniting deep in her belly as desire raced through her blood like a west Texas prairie fire. She'd quickly found herself utterly lost in the sensations of Cash's mouth ravishing her wet folds. When he'd used his fingers to separate the swollen petals of her labia hiding her opening, she had to take deep breaths, then bite her lip to keep from begging him to fuck her.

Just before Cash had started sucking her clit into his mouth and biting down on it gently, she met Collin's gaze. He was standing over her, stroking himself. His cock was so huge, she wondered for a moment if she'd be able to take him. But then she completely lost every ounce of focus when Cash had sucked her clit into his mouth, setting off an explosion of pleasure radiating from the depths of her soul. Every muscle had gone rigid before she screamed out Cash's name. He'd kissed his way up her body and pushed his cock deep inside her before the last of the aftershocks had passed and sent her right back over the edge.

When Cash slid his muscular arms under her and pulled her tightly against his chest, pumping into her with long strokes, she'd felt like she truly belonged to him. At that moment, everything in her world had been in perfect synch. His words spoken against her ear were so rough with pleasure, his tone alone had nearly made her come again.

She'd clung to those sweet words during these past months, but maybe he had just been caught up in the moment when he'd rasped, "You are so fucking beautiful and even more so when you are lost in orgasm. Do you have any idea how much we all want you? We've been looking for you our entire lives. Your body pulses around my cock and tries to keep me inside because it recognizes we are soul mates. Raise your arms over your head and grasp the headboard."

When she finally managed to make her arms follow his instruction, he groaned as her breasts pressed tighter against his chest. "Don't let go or I'll paddle your beautiful ass, love."

She felt him shift his hips and with each thrust, the head of his cock grazed a spot inside her that sent out pulses of pure white-hot energy. His next words sent her over the edge again.

"Come for me, love."

This time when she came, it wasn't as explosive, but it had rocked her to the very foundation of her soul.

Even now, each time she spoke with Cash, she felt as if they had a deep connection. She always felt like he was speaking directly to her heart. Sighing to herself, Layla knew she wasn't going to walk away from them with her heart unscathed, but it was time to face the fact they'd obviously changed their minds. Oh, she knew they still wanted to be her friend, but she wasn't sure she was going to be able to pull that off. Maybe she could until they started seeing someone else. She felt a tear roll down her cheek and cursed herself for letting her mind wander into such a dark place.

Gathering herself up, she plastered on the smile she wore like steel-plated armor, touched up her makeup, and made her way out the door. She'd been living in one of the guest houses behind the Lamonts' spacious home until the manager's apartment was completed at the motel. The apartment wasn't huge, but it was a lot bigger and nicer than any place she'd ever lived. It wasn't a long drive down ShadowDance Mountain into town, but there were a lot of switchbacks that always made Layla nervous.

The first thing she'd done when she got to town was buy a small used car. She still laughed when she remembered the looks on Alex and Zach Lamont's faces when she'd asked for a small advance so she could buy a car. Their tastes in vehicles were much more sophisticated and expensive than hers. They'd readily agreed to give her the advance and had only wanted to know how much she needed. When she'd said six hundred dollars, they'd looked at her as if she'd lost her mind.

Boy, had they put up a fuss when she'd told them she was buying a used subcompact car. Alex had actually paled, and Zach had stood looking at her with his mouth gaping open, blinking in disbelief at her for long moments. Now that she'd gotten to know them better, she understood how significant that moment had actually been.

A few weeks later when she'd told Kat, Jenna, Tori, and Rissa about it during one of their 'rita parties, she'd thought the women were going to fall out of their chairs, they'd laughed so hard. Thinking back on it, she understood how absurd the whole scene had been even though it hadn't seemed all that funny at that moment.

Damn, that had been a fun night with her new friends. How they'd all gotten so giddy when their drinks had been virgin had amazed her. There were several among them who were either pregnant or were trying to get pregnant, so it had just been easier to make all the drinks alcohol-free.

Letting her thoughts wander back to her bosses' frustration over her choice of cars, she reached over and patted the cracked vinyl seat beside her and didn't even try to hold back her giggle. Zach had been much more tactful than Alex, but he'd still tried valiantly to dissuade her despite her insistence the little yellow car was all she could afford. They made her promise she'd trade it for something better before winter or borrow one of their four-wheel-drive SUVs. She'd turned back to thank them one last time before leaving their office and seen Alex Lamont thumping his forehead on his desk, so she'd decided to just leave well enough alone.

Making her way down the steep mountain road, she noticed there was a car following her. It seemed to be gaining on her too quickly, and it flashed through her mind for a split second they weren't going to get shut down in time to avoid rear-ending her. But they'd slowed briefly, flashed their lights a couple of times, then roared past her.

Her eyes had been readjusting after the flashing of their bright lights in her mirrors, so she hadn't gotten a good look at the truck as it roared around her. She did notice it had out-of-state plates, but she hadn't made out anything else. *Crazy asshat was probably in a big hurry to get to the new bar and dance with his two gigantic left feet.*

She found a spot to pull over for a few seconds until her hands stopped shaking, then continued down the steep mountain road into town. By the time she turned into the large parking lot in front of Red Clouds Dancing, she had pushed the unpleasant incident out of her mind. She was determined to enjoy her evening and quickly made her way inside. Her friends had said they'd be here, and she'd asked them to save her a seat. Hopefully, their zaniness would be enough to keep her from slipping into a funk about Cash, Collin, and Clay's change of heart.

Chapter 5

C ASH LET A sigh of relief when Toby sent him a text letting him know he'd just seen Layla's small, yellow POS pull into the lot. The former linebacker was perfect in every way as a bouncer at the bar, and he never missed a chance to give Cash or his brothers shit about the car their woman drove. Hell, it seemed everybody knew she was their woman but the object of their affections. Excusing himself from the table of local city council members he'd been visiting with, Cash sent a quick message to his brothers as he quickly made his way to the entrance.

The minute Layla stepped through the front entrance, he wrapped her in his arms and pulled her against his chest.

"You look beautiful, love. I'm so glad you're here, I was getting worried." He didn't give her time to answer before he turned her into Collin's waiting arms.

"Sweetness, you look gorgeous. I can't wait to get you out on the dance floor." Cash watched as Collin leaned in and whispered against her ear. Cash couldn't hear his brother's words but loved the deep flush that flooded her beautiful cheeks.

Clay was now standing close and pulled her into his arms next. "Baby, you are so beautiful. Will you dance with me after you dance with Cash? I'll get our drinks and be waiting for you. What would you like?"

"I think I'd better stick with iced tea, I'm going to need the caffeine to dance with you later. I've heard about you rodeo cowboys, and I want to be able to keep up." Cash watched as she flirted with Clay—theirs was an easy rapport. He was pleased knowing she'd have a balance with the three of them. He'd spent a lot of time talking with his mom and dads since moving back to Climax.

The one thing his mom had repeatedly cited as a key to their family's success was each of her husbands was different in some significant way. She'd explained when she wanted to joke around, she always sought out Julian, and when she wanted to argue or debate something, she'd go to James. But when she needed guidance or comfort, it was the eldest, Joseph she turned to. She noted she believed he and his brothers would be very similar in strengths and temperaments. And just now, watching how Layla was playful with Clay, Cash could see exactly what his mom had meant.

Cash handed her small handbag to Clay and led his beautiful woman to the dance floor. He looked up at the stage and nodded to the lead singer. The young man immediately launched into Josh Turner's "Soulmate." Cash pulled Layla against him and led her around the floor in a dance he hoped set the stage for an evening of pure seduction. He and his brothers had spent a lot of time planning each and every detail, intending to show her exactly how much they wanted her. They planned to make it perfectly clear simple friendship was *not* their goal.

Remembering how he'd made sweet love to her that night so many weeks ago in Houston, then watched as Collin and Clay had taken her together, he could hardly wait until they had her naked between them again. When Collin had rolled her to her hands and knees and slid deep into her pussy, Clay had guided her lips to his own raging need. Cash had watched as his brothers had brought Layla to the edge of release twice before sending her into a screaming orgasm that had been just about the sexiest thing he'd ever seen.

Bringing his thoughts back to the present, he pulled her up against his rigid length then let his words spill over the shell of her dainty ear. "Feel that, love? That's how much I want you. Never doubt it. But know this—I want all of you.

"I want your sweet smile, your generous spirit, your giving heart, *and your future.*" He caught her as she missed a step in their dance and made the most of the opportunity, pressing her breasts tightly against his chest. "I'll always catch you, love. You can trust me to *always* catch you, so don't ever be afraid to take a leap of faith."

He set her back just enough so he could look into her eyes, wanting to make certain she understood he'd spoken from his heart. He saw tears pool in her emerald eyes, so he knew she had recognized his sincerity.

"Don't cry, love. Please never doubt how much we all care for you. We've made a mistake letting so much time go by, but we knew you were working so hard—hell, we've all been working too hard—and we let our priorities slip. That stops—*now.* After tonight, you'll no longer have to worry we don't want you."

The song had ended, and when she started to speak, Cash placed his fingers over her lips and simply shook his head, then moved his hands to her shoulders and slowly turned her so she was facing Clay.

CLAY HAD CHOSEN "I Swear" by John Michael Montgomery because he wanted Layla to understand how strong his commitment would always be. There wasn't any question he'd been with a lot of women—he'd had his share of buckle bunnies at every rodeo and exhibition stop on the road. Despite his regret, there wasn't a thing he could do to change the past—but he could damned well build a future with the amazing woman dancing in his arms across the planked floor.

It had been his idea to use the old wood from the barn as the dance floor. Once it had all been nailed into place, they'd poured high gloss-high impact poly by the drums full over the top, and the result was astonishingly gorgeous. The poly manufacturers had offered to reimburse them for all their expenses if Red Clouds Dancing would allow them to use the idea in advertising. By Clay's estimation, the free advertising Red Clouds was going to get would make all the work worthwhile.

He smiled down at Layla when she asked him what he was thinking about that had him "grinnin' like the cat that got the canary." He told her about the floor, and she nearly caused a domino effect of wrecked couples when she stopped and dropped down to check it out right in front of the band. He'd quickly lifted her back into his arms, laughing out loud at her outrageous antics.

"Baby, you are somethin' else, you know that? Damn, you are gorgeous, smart, and funny. And you are perfect for us. I want you to know how happy I am you're our woman. I could hold you in my arms like this forever and never get tired of it."

He let the music carry them around the floor. He wanted her to be as comfortable as possible before he pushed her just a bit further. Leaning closer to her and pressing his hard cock against her belly, he whispered right behind her dainty ear.

"Baby, I'd like you to consider coming home with us tonight. I know you can feel how much I want you. We won't push you to make love with us if you aren't ready, but we've done some things with the house we'd like to show you. And since we all have the day off tomorrow, we'd like to spend it with you." He pulled back to look into her eyes just as the song started to wind down. When he saw tears glistening in her eyes, his heart sunk. "Oh, baby, please don't cry. You don't have to come if you don't want to, we'll still want—"

He didn't get to finish because she threaded her fingers through his hair and pulled his face down to kiss him. He knew he should keep the kiss gentle and let her take the lead, but at his first taste of her, all rational thought fled. All he could think about was getting closer and sweeping his tongue over every inch of her sweet mouth.

When he heard someone to the side clear their throat, he realized exactly how out of control his reaction had been. Christ, they were still standing in the middle of the dance floor, and he'd been ready to start stripping her. When he pulled back slightly, he was panting, and once the blood stopped rushing through his ears like a freight train, he could hear the hoots and hollers from their Shadow-Dance friends who were currently taking up three tables at the edge of the floor.

"I have to get back to work, babe, but I'll be checking on you. Enjoy your dance with Collin." He turned her into his brother's arms, then turned to their friends giving them a salute in acknowledgment of their support.

COLLIN HAD BEEN thrilled to see their woman pull his brother down into a kiss so searing, he'd worried Clay was going to fuck her right in the middle of the dance floor. He'd been chosen to go last because he was the one who ordinarily was the most intimidating. They'd hoped by letting Cash and Clay lay the groundwork, his plan for Layla would cinch her going home with them. He looked down and smiled at her slightly dazed look.

"Dance with me, sweetheart." When the band started playing the song he'd chosen for her, Rod Stewart's "Have I Told You Lately," he pulled her into his embrace and started dancing.

He ran his hand in slow circles over her lower back and felt her melt against him—molding her curves to his length. Everything about holding her in his arms felt right, and he didn't want to ever let her go. Collin knew full well the effect his voice had on Layla, and he intended to use that information shamelessly tonight.

Leaning down, so his breath brushed over her soft skin, he started to sing the first refrain. "Have I told you lately that I love you? It's true, there's no one else above you, and you do fill my heart." He kept them moving around the crowded dance floor and was continually finding ways Layla chased away the loneliness he'd felt his entire life.

"It's true, you know. I love you as do both of my brothers. And I want you in ways I hadn't even realized were possible." He felt his friends closing ranks around them, just as they'd planned. Alex was dancing with Katarina, and from the look on her face, his friend was telling his little fireball wife many of the same things Collin was whispering to Layla.

Colt Matthews was dancing with his very pregnant wife, Jenna Lamont-Matthews, and Trace and Tori Bartell were also staying close. Their friends were essentially a shield for Layla as Collin continued to tell her exactly how he wanted to slide his throbbing cock deep inside her glistening pussy.

He wanted her to know the feel of her vaginal walls gripping his cock as he slid in and out of her heat had to be a glimpse of what heaven would be like. When he felt her breathing coming in short panting breaths, he slid his knee between her legs and pressed against her clit.

"Come for me, sweetheart."

He felt her body stiffen and quickly covered her mouth with his, catching her cries of release. It was a good thing he'd had his arm wrapped firmly around her because he felt her knees give way, but to her credit, she recovered quickly and only missed a couple of steps in their dance.

When the song ended, Collin noticed Katarina, Jenna, and Tori all looked like their men had taken them on the same ride, but since each of them was experienced with at least some level of open play at The Club, he knew they wouldn't be intimidated by having an orgasm in public. He led Layla to the edge of the floor and turned her back into his arms.

"Come home with us, sweetheart. Let us love you. Let us show you how great we can be together." Her voice was shaky, but he certainly loved her answer.

"Yes, I... well, I'd like that very much."

He lowered his lips to hers and kissed her with a sense

of urgency that would have left no doubt in her mind how much her answer pleased him. Pulling back, he whispered, "Come on, sweetness, I'll walk you to the restroom and let you freshen up a bit before we join our friends." When they reached the door, he assured her he'd be waiting right there when she returned.

After she had disappeared inside, he sent a quick text to his brothers, making sure they knew she had agreed to go home with them. Even though this was Red Clouds Dancing's grand opening, they'd actually been open for almost a week, so their assistant managers were well-trained and had been quick to offer to close up shop, so the three of them were free to leave earlier than usual tonight. Once the crowd thinned out, they'd be making their way the short distance to their home.

As soon as his parents decided to move to Denver and leave their spacious home for their sons, Collin had started drawing up plans for renovations and improvements. One of the first changes he'd made to those plans after meeting Layla was to add a well-appointed playroom in the basement. He could hardly wait to show it to her, but that wasn't on the agenda for this weekend. This first visit was about showing her the more mainstream changes they'd made to their childhood home.

Cash and Clay had joined him by the time Layla opened the restroom's door and walked out. Her eyes went wide at the sight of all three of them waiting for her and hesitated for just a moment before walking into Cash's open arms.

"I'm keeping you from your guests. This is your big night, you all should be out there greeting your customers and enjoying yourselves. I'm sorry I took so long, but I had to… well, I had to…"

Collin watched as Cash laughed and pulled her chin up from her chest and smiled at her embarrassment.

"Love, we know exactly what Collin did to you on the dance floor. Clay and I are thrilled you trusted him enough to let him take you there. Don't be embarrassed, I'm sure you probably heard from some of your new friends they had similar experiences, didn't you?" Her eyes got absolutely huge, and Collin knew the conversation in the ladies' room must have been very interesting.

"Well... yes, it was mentioned. But they are so much braver than I am about this kind of thing. I'm sassy, but I really don't have that much experience." Cash watched her eyes drop to the floor again and was certain she hadn't intended to share that much information.

Collin stepped forward and lifted her chin. "You were a dream come true, sweetheart. Now, let's get you something to drink, shall we?"

They led her to where the Lamonts, Matthews, Bartells, and Marshalls were holding court at tables they'd pulled together. Their rowdy area quickly became the focal point of the bar and grill, and the Red Clouds were thrilled with their new business's success, but when Collin looked at both of his brothers, he knew they were every bit as anxious as he was to get Layla home and to themselves.

They spent the rest of the evening enjoying the company of their friends, and Collin was relieved to see Layla relax and enjoy herself. He and his brothers made a conscious effort to ensure at least one of them was touching her at all times. As Doms, both he and Cash understood the importance of tactile bonding.

Collin smiled to himself because even though Clay swore he wasn't a natural Dom, he certainly understood on a subconscious level how important it was that their woman was well grounded in their touch. The way she leaned into their touch and never moved away told Collin she'd have suffered a lot from her years of living alone. She always seemed reluctant to answer questions about her family, but they had found out even though her family was in Houston, she'd rarely seen them.

He and his brothers talked extensively about how anxious they were for Layla to meet their mother and fathers. It would be great for her to see how they'd been raised. They wanted her to see that relationships like the one they wanted with her were not only possible, but they'd grown up with it. Seeing their parents example would help with the doubts everyone expected her to experience. He was also anxious for her to meet Lainy, the youngest Red Cloud sibling who was planning to move home within the next month. All of her brothers were anxious to get their beautiful sister back under their protective wings.

Ilaina Red Cloud had become an extremely successful model as she'd finished her college education and gotten her master's degree in advertising and marketing. She'd never viewed modeling as a career though—for her, it had only been a way to make money for school. He was sure the photographers she'd worked with for the past couple of years were giving her the hard sell to stay, but so far, it sounded as if she was holding her own.

Lainy had always been particularly close to Cash, and Collin knew his older brother was anxious for their little sister to make her way home. They'd already built her an entire suite of rooms as an addition to their family home. She'd have the equivalent of her own luxurious apartment, but she'd still be close enough they could look after her without smothering her... hopefully.

Collin glanced toward the bar and immediately zeroed

in on the shaggy-haired man standing at the end, casually leaning with his back to the bar, elbows propped up. His pose was one of what could only be called "intentional nonchalance," and there was something familiar about him Collin couldn't place. Just as he was trying to puzzle it out, he heard Cash's quiet curse, "Fuck. Noah Drummond." And just like that, all of Collin's positive thoughts about how they'd paved the way for Lainy's smooth return home dissipated into a mist of steam like a drop of water onto a hot skillet—unfortunately, it was likely more of a premonition than a poetic observation.

Chapter 6

"WHEN DID HE get home?" Cash asked as he leaned toward Collin. "And how long is he going to be here?" Cash had to work hard not to growl the questions. None of them had ever known exactly what had gone down between their younger sister and the one man who had always seemed to be able to unsettle their normally unflappable sibling. But one thing was for sure, he was the kryptonite she continually tried to avoid.

Noah Drummond was a world-renowned photographer, but Cash was convinced there was something else going on with him. Call it gut instinct, but something had always told Cash there was an undercurrent of danger surrounding Drummond. Deciding to set aside his worries about Noah for now, he refocused his attention on Layla. The last thing he needed was for her to think he was distracted again. And while the situation with Drummond had what his SEAL team referred to as SNAFU—situation normal, all fucked up—written all over it, he would just have to remember to talk to Alex and Zach sometime this next week and find out if they knew what had gone down between Lainy and Drummond several years earlier.

Alex must have followed his line of sight because he spoke quietly, his words directed at Cash and Collin. "He moved back permanently a few weeks ago, I'm surprised he's flown under your radar this long. He's already close to finishing his extensive renovations of the old mill south of the tracks. It's going to be a spectacular studio and gallery."

Cash's expression must have changed because Alex held up his hand to keep him from speaking. "I know you are worried about Ilaina, but she is a full-grown woman and is perfectly capable of taking care of herself. I also know Noah has settled down a lot in the past few years as well." Alex had paused and looked at each of them before zeroing in on Cash.

"You can't micromanage everything—take it from the king of micromanagement. I'm not saying you shouldn't ask questions and stay alert because God knows Zach and I certainly wish we had done a better job with Jenna. I just want you to tread carefully because you are now dealing with two adults who have successfully traveled the world, so it's doubtful either of them will be terribly receptive to you or your brothers' interference." Alex gave him a sympathetic look, and even though he knew his friend was right, it was still going to be hard for Cash to step back completely.

Cash looked at Layla who was looking at him with worry in her eyes rather than the comfort and desire that had been there just a few moments ago. When she leaned close and whispered, "Is everything alright? Do you need me to go so you can get back to work?" his decision was easy. He needed to focus on the treasure sitting next to him. She was his future and deserved his undivided attention. Worrying about Ilaina was for another day.

"No, love. You need to stay right where you are, and I need to stop worrying about things I can't change." He brushed his finger over her soft cheek as he cupped the side of her face. Cash wanted to howl in triumph when she turned her face into his hand and kissed his palm.

"I wasn't trying to eavesdrop, but I overheard your conversation, and I think you're an amazing man to be so concerned for your sister. I hope she knows how lucky she is to have you."

Layla's words touched a part of his heart he'd so often worried was going dormant. The things soldiers see in times of war change them in ways outsiders can rarely grasp. But knowing Layla saw through all the harsh realities of a retired SEAL to the man beneath warmed him as nothing else ever had.

He wasn't sure he could answer around the lump that had formed in his throat, so he just pulled her onto his lap and kissed her, hoping he could make her feel how much she'd touched him. Sweeping his tongue over her lips, he captured her groan as she leaned closer, pressing her soft curves against his chest. Her nipples quickly peaked to sharp points, and he could feel them pressing into his flesh through their clothing. When he finally withdrew his lips from hers, he was pleased to see desire had returned and was now laced with unmistakable lust.

Feeling his hard cock pressed up against her ass was almost more than he was going to be able to resist. He glanced at Collin, hoping his brother would recognize his need and was pleased when he took one of Layla's tiny hands in his and pulled her toward him.

"Come to me, sweetness, big brother needs to share." She quickly slid back onto her own chair and leaned in to kiss him. Cash laughed when Collin growled, picked her up, and moved her skirt out of the way before he deposited her on his lap.

"Oh no, I don't think so. I want you right here where I can feel that sweet ass pressing against me. I want to feel the heat of your pussy through that thong you're wearing. And I want to be able to press my chest against your breasts and feel your nipples peak for me."

Cash smiled at her shocked expression.

"How do you know I'm wearing a thong?"

Collin leaned forward and whispered to her, and Cash would have given anything to know what his brother had said that had caused her to gasp and blush so bright, she nearly glowed in the dimly lit room. He didn't have to wait long to figure it out though when she slowly parted her knees. Collin turned her slowly, so her back was to his chest, then used his own knees to push hers even further apart. Cash and Clay shifted in their chairs, just enough to block the view of others at neighboring tables—there wasn't any need to block anyone at their tables because most of the other women were or had been in similar positions during the evening.

LAYLA HAD BEEN completely overwhelmed by the Red Cloud brothers' attention since the moment she'd walked in the door. It was as if someone had flipped a switch. They'd gone from casual to flaming overnight, and she was still a bit confused by the whole thing but wasn't about to look a gift horse in the mouth either. Having all their sexy attention focused on her was a gift indeed.

She'd watched the interaction of their friends at the tables they'd commandeered and enjoyed the easy camaraderie that seemed to prevail. Everything had been going fine until Cash had looked up at the bar and begun muttering about the guy standing off by himself. The man didn't look much older than she was, and his blond, golden surfer look was a sharp contrast to the three Red Cloud brothers currently surrounding her. The minute they'd started talking about the man, she'd realized Cash's concerns about the man were related to his younger sister, Lainy.

Each of the men had talked to her about their younger sister, but it had been easy to see that it was Cash who had the strongest relationship with the young woman. After they'd spoken about her, Layla had Googled the young woman and been completely stunned to learn the model simply known as "Ilaina" was, in fact, Ilaina Red Cloud.

Layla had been surprised to learn the woman whose face had been on nearly every magazine cover in the world during the past couple of years was moving to Climax to establish her business. From what Layla had read, the young woman was quickly establishing herself as an advertising and marketing genius. The fact that she had chosen to do most of her work away from the more traditional centers for that type of commerce was garnering her even more attention.

In one interview, Ilaina had spoken candidly about the politics of large city ad agencies and why she felt she would be able to provide her clients with much more personalized service if she weren't hindered by the social obligations which accompanied working for a larger agency.

Layla remembered thinking every single quote in the interview was a well-choreographed public relations sound bite and had been impressed with the way Ilaina had managed both the interview and the interviewer. Each time the man had tried to direct the questions to her modeling career, she had skillfully redirected him to her *passion*, which was advertising. The only time Ilaina had seemed to stumble was when she'd been asked why she'd never worked with a photographer named Noah Drummond.

When Cash had called the man at the bar by that name, Layla began listening more closely. She heard Alex Lamont's words of caution and was even more curious now. Then it had occurred to her Cash probably needed to be mingling with his clientele, so he'd have a chance to approach the young man. But when she'd mentioned leaving, so he could get back to work, Cash had seemed to snap out of whatever had derailed his attention. He'd made it clear he didn't want her to leave with a kiss so smoldering, she'd felt the beginning tingles of an orgasm. Cash Red Cloud's kisses were the stuff of her hottest erotic romance novels.

Sitting on Cash's lap had been a mixed blessing because even though she enjoyed being close enough to feel the steely length pressing against her pussy, it made her want to rub her throbbing clit against the denim-covered cock pulsing against her bottom. In a heartbeat, she'd gone from wanting to leave so he could get back to work to a bone-deep desire to strip and drop her needy sex right on top of his cock.

When Collin positioned her on his lap after telling her exactly how he planned to run his fingers over the wet lips of her labia and fuck her with his fingers right there at the table, Layla felt her face heat and worried she might well start glowing, her face was so hot.

Layla felt herself shudder when Collin pulled her back against his chest and parted her thighs with his own as he slid his hands up under her skirt. She noticed the other women at their tables sitting in similar positions during the evening and just now realized why they'd suddenly gotten quiet for long minutes. *Holy fucking mothballs in Memphis if he'd just slide those fingers a little further forward…*

When she tried to shift her hips forward, he spoke against her ear, "Hold still, sweetness. This is my show, you'll get your release, but on my timetable, not yours. Now be a good girl and just lean back and let me play a bit."

Feeling his fingers over the top her lacy thong had been enough to make her completely soak the lace with her cream, but when he pulled the lace aside, and they were skin to skin, she barely contained her moan. Watching as Cash and Clay shifted to block the view of her spread legs from the tables surrounding theirs, she realized just how incredible it could be having the three of them working together for her pleasure. She was starting to lose herself in the sensations when Collin asked, "Would you like to come, sweetheart?"

All she could do was pant out a quick, "Yes…please."

"Because you have been such a good girl and you asked so sweetly, I'm going to give you exactly what your body yearns for." When someone at the next table shouted a greeting to a friend walking by, she was brought back to the reality of where they were and started to struggle to sit up. Knowing she must look wanton, she was suddenly self-conscious.

"Stop. You are beautiful, and you are doing exactly what pleases me. Look at Katarina—look carefully, sweetness. See how she is sitting? Where do you suppose Zach's cock is at this very moment? I can tell you, it's buried deep in his wife's sheath. She doesn't care who sees because her entire focus is on pleasing him."

Layla knew she'd let out a small gasp, partly because she could clearly see that he was right, but also because watching the two lovers fuck right in front of their friends was about the hottest thing she'd ever seen. She hadn't realized she'd spoken out loud until he responded.

"Yes, it is hot to watch, but while everyone at our table knows what they are doing, she's being protected from the view of outsiders by Alex and Colt. You'll soon learn the Doms at The Club work together to ensure their women's safety and pleasure. And even though Colt isn't touching Kat directly, he's contributing to her pleasure just the same."

Layla felt herself begin to relax, leaning back against his chest once again. Now his words felt even more intimate because they were spoken against the sensitive spot just behind her ear.

"See how she trusts her Doms? She knows without looking, they are protecting her even while they provide for her pleasure. See how the muscles in her arm are flexing in a rhythmic pattern? Those flexes are in time with her pussy's contractions. She is milking Zach's cock with a strength you can be sure is going to bring them both to a breath-stealing release. Watch, and you'll see the depth of their love for each other and their commitment to one another's pleasure wash over their faces."

Just as his words moved through her mind, Layla saw Kat's head fall back against Zach's shoulder, and Alex leaned over and sealed his mouth over hers in what looked like a kiss, but Layla knew he used the moment to capture Kat's cries of release. Zach's body went perfectly still, then his forearm tightened under Kat's breasts, and Layla was sure he'd found his own release buried in his wife's soft-ness. It was one of the most erotic things she'd ever witnessed, and for just a moment, she was jealous of the love she saw shining in the eyes of all three Lamonts.

Layla lost herself in the feeling of Collin's touch, and

when he began circling her aching clit, she wanted to cry out with her need.

"Relax for me, sweetheart. Let me take you there. Trust me to give you what your sweet body craves. Don't come yet, hold off for me. It'll be sweeter, I promise you."

She thought he'd lost his mind—how was she supposed to delay what felt like a wave of desire so deep, it was threatening to pull her out to sea? Layla could only nod her head because it was taking every bit of her concentration just to keep from crying out. When he pushed two fingers in deep, she was grateful Clay leaned over, taking her lips in a heated kiss because she'd lost the battle she'd been waging to keep quiet. Collin pumped his fingers in and out of her soaking heat, and she hoped others at the table weren't able to hear the wet sound of him fucking her with his fingers. Just as she was starting to worry, Collin pinched her clit and whispered against her ear.

"Come for me, sweetheart. Come all over my fingers, lose yourself in your pleasure. Clay will catch your cries and lock them in his heart."

Collin's words of encouragement were all she needed, and the minute he'd told her to come, she let go and was grateful Clay had indeed captured her keening cry as wave after wave of pleasure washed over her. Collin's groans sent her pleasure higher again, and she felt a second flood of cream leave her body in a heated rush. As she started to come back to earth, she heard Collin's growled words.

"Christ, let's get her home before I fuck her on the table in front of God and everybody."

Suddenly, all three men were moving. Collin pushed her skirt back in place, and she was once again sitting on his lap in what looked affectionate, but not particularly intimate. When Clay lifted her to her feet, she was thankful he pulled her against his side when she wobbled, and her knees threatened to give way.

"Hang on, baby, we're going to get you out of here before we all do something in front of half the town that will have Mom's Ladies Aid pals calling her first thing tomorrow morning. And while our mama is mighty open-minded, as you'd expect someone with three husbands would be, she wouldn't be happy if we stripped you and took our pleasure for everyone to see."

He held her while Cash and Collin said their goodbyes and gave the staff last-minute instructions. She could feel Clay's cock pressing against her lower back. It was humbling to realize she'd been given two mind-blowing orgasms, but she hadn't given them any way to find their own release.

Cash moved in front of her and lifted her chin with his fingers, so he was looking directly into her eyes. "Love, where are your keys? We'll have one of the guys bring your car over after they close the bar." When she started to argue, he simply shook his head and continued, "You are in no condition to drive, love, and besides, we want to have your softness pressed against us as we make our way home. Now, are your keys in your purse, beautiful?" She nodded and handed him her small bag.

He opened the bag and smiled at her with a grin that made her instantly remember the last thing she'd added to her purse before walking out the door.

"Nice to know we were all on the same page, love," was all he said before removing her keys and handing the small bag back to her.

Chapter 7

LAYLA WAS WARM, sandwiched between Cash and Clay in the front seat of Cash's large truck. At the last minute, Collin had opted to drive her small car to their place since it had been starting to snow. He told her he didn't want anyone from the bar driving any more than necessary at that late hour.

Layla was relieved the small car would be moved before there was much snow. She knew her tires weren't the best and was worried about someone driving it later. Cash's truck rounded the corner, and she caught sight of their home and gasped in surprise.

Even though they lived close to the motel and dance club, the house itself was around a bend and mostly hidden by several rows of tall pines, so she'd never seen it up close. The entire structure was awash in soft lights. The natural rock front highlighted rounded archways as the focal points of a porch that looked like it wrapped around at least three sides of the large home, making it look more like an elaborate citadel-style adobe than a ranch home.

"Oh my God, your home is amazing. You must be so proud of it. I'll bet my entire apartment would have fit in your entryway, am I right?" She smiled at Cash because he'd seen her apartment in Houston and had been none too impressed with either the neighborhood or her living conditions.

"Well, love, I don't know about the entryway, but it would certainly fit in the master bath."

He grinned at her and even though she knew he was probably serious, she appreciated him keeping the conversation light, so she didn't take offense. Layla knew at that moment, a man who would consider her feelings even while teasing would steal her heart if she wasn't careful. *Right... like it isn't already a done deal.*

Clay helped her out of the truck, just as Collin stomped his way toward them.

"Sweetheart, I love you, and I'm only going to say this once. That car is not safe for man or beast, and it's certainly not safe enough for our woman. It is not to be moved from where it sits until I can have it towed from here. It's almost—shit, what's the next fucking holiday? Oh, right, it's almost Thanksgiving, so you'll be getting a new vehicle for a Thanksgiving gift." He kissed her on the forehead, then said, "Come on inside, it's freezing out here."

They all took off walking, and she just stood there stunned. *What the ever-loving fuck? He can't just decide I need a new car. I can't take a gift like that, good gads.*

When the three men finally realized she wasn't with them, they all turned at once and looked back at her. She fisted her hands on her hips and glared.

"Are you serious? You can't do that!" She knew her voice would have sounded much more sincere if she hadn't been shivering in the cold, but she tried to make up for her lack of volume by adding in a good dose of attitude.

"Exactly when did you get to be the king of my kingdom, Collin? I don't remember abdicating my throne to you." She looked up and saw Clay's grin just as she heard Collin growl. The next thing she knew, she was hanging upside down over Collin's shoulder as he stalked toward the house.

"We'll discuss this inside where it's warm—when you're naked. It's just a hunch, but I'm betting you'll be a lot more cooperative when you're naked, and I'm sliding my cock in and out of your sweet pussy."

Damn it, as much as she wanted to be offended, she wasn't. When she felt her pussy start to cream, she didn't doubt for a moment Collin would be able to smell her arousal since it was right up there by his fracking nose. As her new friend, Kat would say, damn and double damn.

Collin set her on her feet as soon as they got in the front door, and she swayed on her feet when all the blood rushed from her head. Cash stepped forward and steadied her. "Careful, love—we don't want to fall."

Collin stood in front of her with his arms crossed over his chest and Cash chuckled. "Collin seems pretty determined your little car isn't safe, beautiful. It seems I recall you made a deal with Alex and Zach about that car, didn't you?"

"Yeah, I know. I promised I'd get rid of it before it snowed, but it really hasn't snowed *a lot* yet, and I've been trying to eke out the last of the use on the tires, you know? I just don't have much money saved up yet to buy anything better." She was suddenly feeling very vulnerable with all of them staring at her like she was some kind of errant school girl who was refusing to listen to reason.

Layla had been poor all her life and not having money in her savings account these past couple of years made her feel unsettled. She needed to know she had a safety net because her uncle wouldn't be in prison forever, and when he was finally released, she was going to have to start running... and that would take money.

Cash leaned forward and looked at her intently. "What were you thinking about just then?" When she dropped her eyes to the floor, he leaned closer and pulled her chin up, so she was forced to look at him. "Eyes on mine, beautiful. Now answer my question. I'll caution you not to lie because I will know. Also, lying by omission is still lying, just in case you think leaving out critical information might work out for you."

Layla took a deep breath and sighed. "I was just thinking about how uncomfortable I've been not having any money in savings. I've always struggled with money, well, ever since my family sent me out on my own when I was… well, I was pretty young, let's just go with that. As for the rest of it… it's a really long story, and I promise to tell you everything, but I'm not really ready to go there just yet. Is that okay? I don't want to lie, but I'm just not ready to have this conversation yet." She felt tears burn her eyes, but she blinked furiously, determined to hold them back.

Layla watched Cash as he considered her words, struck by the fact he hadn't gotten angry, but there was something in his eyes she could only think of as disappointment, and that tore at her heart.

She blurted out, "I'm sorry. I don't mean to hurt you. It's just that, well, I didn't want tonight to be about that." She kept her eyes on his and knew when he accepted her words because the lust returned to his expression in a rush. Relieved more than she could say, she let out a breath and leaned against his chest.

"Thank you for understanding. I want to get back to that really nice place where you all wanted me. Can we save the *issues* for later?"

Cash had wrapped his arms around her, and she was overwhelmed by the feeling she could conquer the world with him in her corner. For the first time since her uncle had been led screaming out of the courtroom, she wondered if she might be able to make a stand against him and survive it.

Finally, she reluctantly pulled back and looked up into Cash's heated gaze. She didn't know the words to tell him how much she wanted him. All she could think to do was to put her hands on either side of his face and pull him down into a sweet kiss. He moved his hand to her ass and pressed her tighter against his rigid length, making her moan as need swamped her. Layla could have sworn the energy in the room began to sizzle and snap as it shifted.

Cash lifted her, and she easily wrapped her legs around his lean hips. She felt him walking and knew instinctively Collin and Clay were following them, but she wasn't paying any attention to which direction they'd moved or how far they'd gone. She only came back to awareness when her bare ass cheeks met cold marble. She gasped out a small screech of surprise.

"Oh, my stars and garters that's cold. Why did you... holy fracking fairy farts... where are we? This room is amazing."

"This is the master bath, love," Cash smiled down at her. "Do you like it? We're all going to enjoy a nice warm shower before we go to bed, how does that sound?"

Layla watched as Clay stepped up to what looked like a control panel that could probably launch a space shuttle. He started pressing buttons, and she didn't have any idea what they could all possibly be for. He must have sensed her questions because he stepped back and smiled.

"It's really very user-friendly, and we'll be happy to show you how to run the sound system, water temperature and pressure controls, the lighting, and the glass frosting—but not until later—hopefully, much later." He winked at her, and she felt her heart lighten. Clay always seemed to know exactly when she needed that little bit of fun to take the edge off an emotionally charged situation.

Layla watched as Collin effortlessly stripped off his clothing. She knew she was staring at his roped muscles, but she didn't much care if her mouth was hanging open. Each of the Red Cloud brothers was a picture of male perfection. Their golden-brown skin and muscular bodies were practically works of art. Each had the same blue-black hair which shone under the overhead lights.

Collin and Cash were both over six-feet-tall and leaner than Clay. The youngest of the brothers was five feet eleven, and his broader shoulders and muscular back were a testament to his bull riding days. She also knew he'd spent the past weeks dividing his time between their parents' ranch and the carpentry work he'd done at the dance club.

Cash stepped back to remove his clothes, and Collin moved in front of her. He grasped her fingers and pulled her slowly to her feet.

"You have too many clothes on, sweetness." He paused and seemed to be studying her... waiting for something, but she wasn't sure what.

She felt herself being drawn into his heated gaze and wanted to please him more than she wanted her next breath. The thought was humbling because it was a direct reflection of everything Tori and Kat had told her about submissives during a discussion one night as they'd enjoyed a glass of tea. They'd been lounging by the waterfall in the gardens behind the Lamonts' beautiful home chatting, and the other women had told her about their chosen lifestyle.

Layla had tried to explain she just wasn't able to wrap

her mind around the concept, and they'd both laughed. Their assurance she'd understand it clearly when the moment arrived had seemed hollow until this moment.

"Sweetheart, I don't know where you went just now, but I'd say it had something to do with a flash of enlightenment. Did you just have an 'aha' moment?" She heard the slight teasing tone in his voice and appreciated he was trying to ease back into her good graces after their little confrontation by the front door.

"Yes, I did. It was something Tori and Kat mentioned, but I didn't understand it until now. They said I'd get it, but I didn't really believe them." She could hear her voice had become breathy and sounded needy even to her own ears.

Collin smiled and leaned forward so he could ask his question against her neck. "Your desire to please us surprises you, doesn't it?"

"How did you know?" She knew her eyes had gone wide and she felt her jaw fall open.

By this time Cash had returned to her. "We've both been Doms for a long time, love." He chuckled when she looked confused. "Hope you don't play poker, beautiful because you have a very expressive face. What I mean is we've talked to a lot of subs. We've trained both Doms and subs, so we know the signs of an epiphany when we see them."

Collin added, "Some of the most intelligent, driven, and successful women I know are submissives. They relish their time with their Doms because all they have to do is feel. They aren't responsible for the jobs of the people working for the corporations or businesses they own and/or operate. They don't have to worry about how their actions are going to impact the company's stock, nor do they need to worry about what some asshole board member is going to dream up to bitch about. Having a time when they have no responsibility other than pleasing their Dom is freeing for them. Is that close to what they told you? Because they are both very intelligent and successful women, so I'm sure they have each experienced something similar."

She was so surprised by his words, all she could do was nod. Clay seemed to sense her need to step back for a bit and spoke up.

"Let's get our girl into the shower and show her all the great things that can happen on the other side of that door. Come on, baby, time for water sports." He waggled his eyebrows at her, and when he extended his hand, she let him pull her closer to the now steaming shower.

Cash stepped up behind her and stripped her bare in seconds. Feeling the air over her recently waxed pussy caused her nipples to draw up into tight buds, and she felt cream rushing to coat her folds.

Clay paused to look at her appreciatively. "You are so fucking gorgeous. You take my breath away, baby girl. Our grandmother always taught us to respect the wisdom of Great Spirit, but I have no idea what it saw in me that could have possibly deserved such a precious gift, but I'll say a prayer of thanks every day for the rest of my life for his insight." She felt tears at the back of her eyes and was relieved when he tugged on her hand and said playfully, "Come on, last one in is a rotten egg."

CLAY RED CLOUD had never had any desire to be a sexual Dominant. He just hadn't ever seen it as who he was as a man. Clay loved women—old, young, short, tall, hell, he loved them all. His mom had always said he took after Dad Julian who she had always said was her charmer. He'd grown up watching as Dad Julian filled a very big role in his mom's life. He was the one she went to when she needed a hug and a giggle, always the one who could make her smile when things had been strained in their home for one reason or another. More than once, he'd heard his mom call him *Niz*. Clay had finally asked why, and she'd told him it was the abbreviated form of *nizhónígo* which was the Navajo word for happiness. Clay had only been in his early teens at the time, but her words had made a lasting impression on him.

When Clay phoned his sweet mama last week, just to hear her voice, he'd mentioned that day to her and been pleasantly surprised she'd remembered every vivid detail. She had gotten quiet and then said, "You were always my sweet boy, and the woman who captures your heart is a lucky woman indeed because you'll bring sunlight and happiness to her life, just as my love Julian has done for me. Clay, never underestimate the importance of your contribution to the family you'll form one day."

He'd heard her sniffle and wished he could pull her into his arms and hug her. As the youngest son, he had always had a particularly close relationship with his mom. His brothers had usually been off with either Dad Joseph or Dad James while he and baby Lainy had been home with their doting mother. In truth, that extra time in her loving care was likely a large part of the reason he tended to be the romantic, playful one, and it was a role he relished.

Right now, he was enjoying the feel of Layla's softness nestled against his strength. She'd lost too much weight since they all moved to Climax. She'd been working so hard, and he knew money had continued to be an issue for her.

Layla had told him she'd had to use up all her savings during her college years, and he knew that had bothered her. When the three of them had noticed the drop in her weight, they'd begun paying very close attention to her eating habits. They'd even watched how often she went grocery shopping which hadn't been nearly often enough. They'd started dropping by with lunches for her, and those had progressed to extended breaks so she could get a little balance back into her life.

Clay pulled her under one of the large shower heads that simulated a soft rain shower. He kissed her while rivulets of water soaked them in a slow drenching avalanche of warm water.

"Have you ever been kissed in the rain, sweetheart?" He grinned at her slightly dazed look. Damn, he loved seeing her eyes clouded with desire. He'd argued long and hard with his brothers about this shower during their renovations and the construction phases of their remodeling project. Clay had believed so firmly in his vision for the master bath, he'd finally offered to cover the entire cost himself if they'd agree to everything he wanted done.

Smiling to himself, he thought about all the fun he was going to have rubbing it in their faces now because the look on Layla's face when she'd stepped into the shower enclosure had made every cent he'd spent worth it. The back wall of the shower was made up of floor to ceiling windows that looked out over the valley—the view was breathtaking in the daylight. The high-carbonate glass could be frosted with the touch of a button if more privacy was desired.

He'd spent hours wandering through the inventory of

regional quarries until he'd found enough of the flat, smooth stones in varying shades of gray and black to make the benches and create the cascading wall of water he'd inlaid with subtle lighting.

The end wall was highlighted by the stone waterfall and also served as the backdrop of the hot tub. When the lights in the room were shut down, the ambiance from the sound of the cascading water and the twinkling of the soft lights transformed the entire room a romantic getaway. The actual bathroom facilities were in a smaller room through a door that most people wouldn't even notice.

The adjoining mistress closet was enormous and had entrances from both the bedroom and this room. Clay had read countless magazines and talked to every woman who would answer his questions about their bathrooms. He smiled to himself when he thought back on the strange looks he'd gotten, but all that input had been worth its weight in gold.

He pulled back from the kiss and smiled at Layla's slightly dazed expression.

"Baby, we want you to just relax and let us take care of you. Can you do that?" When she slowly nodded, he leaned down and kissed her again just as he saw Cash begin running his shampoo-covered hands gently through her long tresses. Clay broke the kiss and whispered into her ear, "Feel how Cash's hands are making love to your hair, baby? Let his hands massage your scalp and imagine how wonderful those hands are going to feel as they move over every inch of your naked body. I promise you, there isn't going to be a single sweet spot we don't worship tonight."

When Layla groaned, he looked down to see Collin's soapy hands smoothing up and down her toned legs. "Col's hands are working their magic on you also aren't they, baby? Feel how he moves with deliberate pacing, so every nerve ending is ignited with need?"

He lowered his head and licked over both nipples before pulling the first one into his mouth with a strong suction that pushed the sensitive tip against ridges lining the roof of his mouth. She arched her back, pushing her ample breasts deeper into his mouth. He showered each breast with attention and could hardly wait until he could hold the mounds tightly together and fuck them until his seed coated her chest and throat. The warrior in his blood was never far from the surface when he was with her, and the need to mark her was pushing itself to the forefront.

"Spread your legs farther apart for Collin, baby. Let him start preparing you for what we have planned." When her breathing hitched, he saw a flash of uncertainty in her eyes. Holding her face to his, he asked, "Do you trust us, Layla? Does your heart know how much we want you and we'd never do anything you didn't want?"

He knew the answer before she responded by the way her pretty emerald eyes softened, and arousal once again replaced the apprehension. Her words were quietly spoken, but they held the future of each man in their sincerity.

"Yes, I trust you... each of you with my body *and my heart.*"

Chapter 8

W HEN CASH HAD heard her soft words to Clay, he nearly stopped breathing. She was so incredibly perfect—it was as if God had custom designed her for the three of them. There was a radiance that shone from her soul, and he wanted nothing more than to spend the rest of his life basking in its warmth. He finished her hair and stepped back, so he could quickly take his own shower.

Hell, if he hadn't been worried about offending her, he'd have given his throbbing cock a couple of good yanks and relieved himself, so when he finally sunk into her, he'd last longer. He was just going to have to master himself because he wasn't taking any chance that might jeopardize what they had planned for her.

Cash wanted their first time in what he considered *her* room and bed to be a memory she would treasure forever. Hopefully, some evening, fifty years from now as they sat out on the front porch, watching their grandchildren play in the yard, she would lean over to each of them and replay this night in a voice that still lifted in excitement as she recalled the memories they'd created.

Once they moved Layla out of the shower, they dried her gently with plush towels warmed in the warmer Clay had insisted they purchase. Clay had mentioned how the hospital staff always brought him warm blankets after he'd been injured and how amazing it felt, so they'd installed one.

Their dads had growled at them when their mother recently insisted they buy her one of the expensive units after she'd used one of their warm towels the last time she'd been home to visit.

Wrapping the towel around Layla had been a sensual moment, and he'd basked in the satisfied feeling he'd gotten from being able to care for her. He wanted to make sure she felt every bit of love they could offer.

Cash had taken the lead the last time they'd been together, so it was important to make sure one of his brothers took that position tonight. Their original plan had been for Collin to step up, but after the two of them had gone toe to toe about the car, they agreed by silent communication to have Clay take his place. For some reason they didn't fully understand, Layla seemed to be in need of a little less harsh direction tonight. Clay would be perfect for getting her to the place where she'd be in the right frame of mind for them to push her boundaries a bit tomorrow. They wanted to spend the weekend in bed but knew their little bundle of energy wouldn't be able to sit still that long.

Clay walked her out of the en suite and into the bedroom, and Cash smiled when she took in the room. They'd heard her talk about her love of books and built her floor-to-ceiling bookshelves, complete with a rolling ladder. Between the shelves was a wide padded window seat where she would have a view of both the front of the house and the woods. The wooded area was bordered by a narrow, fast-moving river. From the raised position of the house, her view would overlook the colorful tapestry of rocks along the riverbed, and in the summer when she opened the windows, she'd be able to listen to the rushing water from the snow melt as she lay in bed.

They'd started working on the house even before they'd met Layla, but this addition had become an obsession after finding her. He knew Collin had orchestrated the stepped-up start of construction on the addition before they'd even left Houston which had told Cash just how much the little blonde had affected his brother. It was rare for Collin to use his money for anything other than building his electronics empire.

Honestly, his brother was one of the people least impressed with his wealth. He'd become a millionaire at twenty-two-years-old and had multiplied that many times over. Their entire family had wondered what it would take to make Collin take an interest in and use some of the money he seemed to have so little regard for, and now they knew—Layla Lang.

"Whose room is this? It's amazing." She might have stopped talking, but Cash watched as she continued looking around, her eyes wide with interest. For just a split second, he got a glimpse of what she must have looked like as a child and a flash of what their own child would look like. He could barely contain his excitement at the thought of her belly round with their child.

Clay smiled and answered, "This is what we call the Mistress Suite, baby. It was built for you, and I can't tell you how happy we are to hear you say you like it." Cash watched his youngest brother brush the backs of his fingers over the curve of her cheeks still flushed pink and dewy from her shower. In a lifetime, he knew none of them would ever get enough of touching her.

When Clay's words registered, she looked at each of them in turn. "What? Why? You didn't even seem to want me until tonight. I don't understand. I thought you had decided that we should just be friends or... well, maybe even something less."

Cash wanted to growl his frustration with the mistakes they'd made with her. It had never occurred to him she would make such an inaccurate assumption when nothing could have been further from the truth. Clay framed her face with his large hands and brought her attention to his face.

"Baby, we'll kick ourselves forever for letting you think something so wrong—and believe me, that observation is about as far from fact as it could get." Sighing he shook his head before continuing, "We knew your new job was important to you and thought we'd give you a little space and time to get settled in. In the meantime, we worked day and night to get Red Clouds up and running. We also worked to complete some major construction and renovation to this house. I assure you, you have been first and foremost in our minds as we considered each change, color choice, and design question. We'll give you the full tour tomorrow, but right now, we have something else in mind."

While he'd been speaking, he'd been slowly leading her toward the bed. Cash knew she hadn't even been aware they'd been moving until Clay turned her gently, and her curvy little ass bumped against the mattress.

Cash and Collin both moved forward, so they flanked Clay as his hands slid inside the silk robe they'd put on her after her shower. The deep emerald fabric clung to her curves and brought out the color of her eyes. It was thin enough her peaked nipples were predominantly on display, and Cash couldn't wait to see how the delicate fabric looked when it was pressed against nipple rings if they could talk her into having them pierced. Clay's hands slowly opened the front of the robe before sending it sliding off her small shoulders, skimming down her back to pool at her feet.

LAYLA HAD NEVER seen a more beautiful bedroom, not even in the magazines she used to look through at the library. After her family had put her out on the street, there hadn't been enough money to actually *buy* magazines or books, so she'd spent long hours at the nearest library. She'd looked at hundreds of periodicals, longing for a home and family like those she saw pictured on their glossy pages.

The bed in this room had to have been custom made because it could easily sleep five or six people. Cripes, where did you even go to buy something that large? The sheets reminded her of the soft blended hues of a Monet painting, the blues and greens melding together in perfect harmony that was highlighted by a sun-drenched yellow. The entire room was done in all her favorite colors, and she wondered how they could have possibly known.

Layla found herself being completely seduced by Clay's voice, touch, and words. She knew Cash and Collin were standing mere inches to the side, but she'd been getting close to feeling overwhelmed, so she was concentrating on Clay.

She liked the way Clay grounded her, but then… she felt that way with each of the Red Cloud brothers when they focused their attention on her. How could she be so drawn to each of them when they really were very different?

When Clay's work-roughened hands slid inside the robe they'd helped her into moments earlier, the pads of his fingers moving over her sensitized nipples, she felt her breath catch. Suddenly realizing she was almost panting with need when the robe slipped to the floor, she glanced at each man and was relieved to see the same raw lust and desire reflected in their gazes. At least she wasn't going down in this deal alone.

Deciding she needed to take a leap of faith and let them know she'd been reading up on poly-relationships, at least what little had been available, she took a steadying breath.

"I've been reading you know... and well, I think I have an idea how this has to work... for us to all be together at the same time."

She felt like all the blood in her body was pooling in her lower regions, and the arousal was sending so much moisture to her pussy, she was starting to worry it would be running down her legs in a few minutes. *Oh yeah, that'll be a real turn-on for them. I swear I'll die of embarrassment if that happens.*

"I... well, I bought a plug... a kind of small one, but I wanted to see if... *geez.* This is beyond embarrassing." She dropped her gaze, suddenly flooded with self-doubt. Why hadn't she kept her mouth shut? Damn it, she was always yakking when she should just keep quiet.

This time it was Collin who spoke. "Sweetheart, you should never be embarrassed by anything you want to say to *any* of us. We'll always do our best to answer your questions and listen to whatever you have to say. Communication is the key to all relationships, but it's absolutely critical when they are polyamorous. As Cash and I teach you more about Dominant/submissive relationships, those communication skills will become even more important.

So please, don't ever feel embarrassed by anything you want to say or ask."

When she looked up at him, she saw nothing but sincerity in his expression, and that gave her self-confidence just the boost it needed. She smiled her thanks and nodded.

"Well, I got a plug, but I think you must have to be some special kind of Olympic gymnast or maybe circus contortionist to get the thing in by yourself." Waving her hand trying to brush the memory of how crazy she must have looked trying to push that damned pick piece of plastic in her ass, Layla tried to smile but doubted she was very convincing.

"So, well... what I wanted to say is, I kept trying because I wanted to be ready in case you changed your minds and wanted me, but then when I couldn't really manage it, and your interest didn't seem to be coming back..." She let her words go unfinished because her heart was clenching at the memory of the nights she'd cried herself to sleep after moving to Climax and getting what had seemed like the brush-off from the three brothers who had rocked her world in Houston before her graduation. Suddenly, all three men were surrounding her, and she heard Cash's harsh voice above the others.

"Fuck, I'll never forgive myself for putting those tears in your eyes, love." Both Collin and Clay made similar statements, and before she realized it, she was on the bed between Clay and Cash. Collin moved to a small cabinet at the foot of the bed, and when he returned, she saw him toss a condom to Clay.

Cash claimed her mouth in a kiss so scorching, it felt like a hot Texas summer wind. She heard the tear of foil just before Clay said, "Come on, baby, ride me." Cash helped lift her, so she was straddling Clay's hips. Feeling the heated steel of his sheathed cock pressing against her slick folds nearly sent her over the edge of release, and suddenly, all she could think about was getting him inside her. She was nearly frantic with the need to feel his cock pressing between her vaginal walls. The need to languish in the sensation of each bump and ridge teasing her sensitive tissues was almost all-consuming.

Layla knew her movements had become jerky and uncoordinated. Her clumsy behavior had to have been a stark contrast to their previous lovers... and wasn't that a depressing thought? Clay must have sensed her desperation because his large hands gripped her forearms, stilling her.

"Baby, I'm not going anywhere, so there is no need to rush. Let us take care of everything. Let us love you."

The relief she felt at his words surprised her, and she found herself unable to speak around the lump that had suddenly taken up residence in her throat. She felt a tear slide down her cheek, and all she could do was nod. He smiled up at her.

"Please tell me those are tears of relief you don't have to do this yourself, baby."

She finally managed a whispered, "Yes, they are. I'm sorry, I was just so... well, I just wanted to feel you inside me so much, I kind of went off the deep end for a minute." Layla leaned forward and kissed him. "Thank you for understanding me when I don't really understand myself right now. All I know is I want you... all three of you with a desperation I don't know how to describe or deal with."

Hoping her honesty wasn't overdone, she looked up at Cash and Collin to find them both smiling at her with indulgent expressions. She let out a breath she hadn't even realized she was holding and leaned over to kiss first Cash, then Collin before leaning forward and pressing a kiss against Clay's lips. When he pulled her closer, the soft hair on his chest teased her taut nipples, and she moaned into the kiss.

The soft sound of her need must have been all the invitation the three men needed because she was immediately besieged by their touch. It seemed like there wasn't any part of her that wasn't being worshipped.

When she felt fingers trailing up her spine, she instinctively arched her back, knowing she'd pushed her ass high in the air, hoping someone took notice because if somebody didn't fuck her soon, she was going to have to resort to begging. Hell, that begging thing sounded like a mighty fine idea now that she gave it a heartbeat of consideration.

"Please... oh, please... I need..."

Collin leaned over her shoulder and asked against her ear, "What do you need, sweetheart? Say the words, and we'll give you exactly what you want."

"I want to find out... if those women on the internet meant what they said." Just then Clay lifted her and slid her back down slowly over his cock, and she threw her head back and groaned at the exquisite sensations. When he was fully seated inside her, she leaned forward, and the neatly trimmed hair above his cock tickled her clit, and she felt her entire body tense in response.

"Oh Jesus Christ, she just clamped down on me like a vise. I'll never last. Get her ready and let's give our woman what she craves before this turns into an eight-second ride."

She could hear the strain in Clay's voice, and if she hadn't been working so hard to control her own responses, she might have had more appreciation for his rodeo humor.

"Damn it, Cash, distract her while Collin gets her ready

for his cock."

She had never felt anything like the sensation of cool gel lube being drizzled over her ass. The way it trailed over her back hole, then slid to her pussy was an erotic tease. When Cash moved forward and held his cock out to her, she saw the pearly drop of pre-cum glistening at the slit and couldn't help but lick her lips in anticipation.

"Oh, love, that was just about the hottest thing I've ever seen. The look on your face and that pink tongue licking your lips were enough to test my control and... oh, holy fuck... I want my cock inside that sweet mouth. That's it—oh Christ that feels unbelievable." She had taken him deep on the first stroke and was thrilled to hear his gasp as his cock jerked in response.

Caressing his cock with her tongue was a feeling she knew she would never get tired of. She wanted to learn every ridge, vein, and bump that made each of them unique. She was lost in the feeling of the head pressing against the back of her throat, and when she lightly grazed her teeth over the base, she heard him shout.

"Fuck! That feels so good. Christ, I can't even think straight. Love, your mouth is going to be the death of me."

She made several more strokes and was so focused on giving Cash a blow job he'd never forget, she hadn't realized how she was arching and pressing her ass against Collin's probing fingers. She heard Collin's words but didn't really take time to process their meaning.

"That's three fingers, sweetheart. Christ, you are so hot, I can't wait to slide my cock inside this sweet ass."

She moaned as he withdrew his fingers, and when she arched again, she felt Clay pull her lower to his chest. She redoubled her efforts, sucking hard on Cash until he was once again fucking her mouth with long, deep strokes.

"Love, I'm going to come if you don't want to swallow me down, let go now."

Let go? Is he insane? I worked hard for this, and I want every drop. She tightened her lips and moaned and was rewarded by his shout and the feeling of his seed coating her throat and tongue. His tangy essence was a gift, and she wasn't about to miss a drop of it.

When Cash pulled his cock from her mouth, he collapsed next to her on the bed, panting. He turned to face her and ran his fingers down the side of her face and smiled at her, his eyes bright with admiration.

"Christ that was amazing, love. I swear you just stole a piece of my soul." He smiled at her and leaned over, kissing her.

Layla felt the head of Collin's cock pressing in, and the burn was just about to make her call a halt when Cash kissed her, and her mind centered on the feeling of Cash's tongue plundering her mouth and Clay's cock pulsing inside her pussy. When Cash pulled back from the kiss, her entire body was vibrating with desire, and she felt like a kid who had just been given carte blanche in a candy store.

Collin stilled her movements. "Christ, Layla, hold still. Don't push back, sweetness, I don't want to hurt you. We have to take this slow or we could—"

Layla had no interest in slow. All she wanted was to feel him deep inside her. Her body was smoldering in need and following his order wasn't even anywhere on her short list of options.

They must have known what she was thinking because both Clay and Collin shouted "No!" just as she sucked in a deep breath and thrust her ass back, deeply impaling herself on Collin's cock. She screamed at the burn and the jolt of pure white lightning that raced up her spine, then back down to light up her clit like a fourth of July fireworks display.

"I'm going to paddle your ass for that, sweetheart—but not until after Clay and I fuck you. Go!" He and Clay set a fast pace, and she was lost. This time, Clay locked his arms around her and held her tightly against his chest as he and Collin alternately pushed in deep and withdrew, so she was always filled. When Collin leaned forward and said, "Come for us, sweetheart," her world exploded into a million pieces of pure white light. Spots danced before her eyes, and she wasn't sure she was going to be able to keep from passing out.

Before she had completely returned to earth, she felt Collin lift her from Clay's chest which sent Clay's cock over her sweet spot. She threw her head back and screamed as she came again. They began thrusting again, and she heard them both shout and felt their cocks stiffen and jerk with their release, but she was so spent, all she could do was fall back onto Clay when Collin released his hold on her.

She didn't know how long she laid draped over Clay in an exhausted heap, but by the time her brain re-engaged, Collin had already pulled from her body, and she became aware that someone was cleaning her with a warm, wet cloth. When she would have jerked away, Clay banded her tightly against his chest again even though he was no longer inside her.

"Let us care for you, baby. It pleases us to do this for you, please don't deny us this pleasure." His words drifted over her like a warm summer breeze, and she laid her head back down on his chest... and that was the last thing she remembered.

Chapter 9

H OLY FUCKING CAT balls, this is what she got for deciding to surprise her three pervert brothers. Lainy knew her brothers were interested in a new woman, hell, she and Cash talked on the phone at least once a week and texted each other almost daily. She was thrilled her brothers had found a woman they all seemed to agree was perfect for them because quite frankly, she hadn't really thought it would be possible. She knew they weren't expecting her until next week, but she had decided to come home and surprise them for the Grand Opening of Red Clouds Dancing. And if her damned flight hadn't been delayed at JFK, she would have made her flight to Denver and been here in plenty of time. The way it was, she'd pulled up just as the last of the staff had been locking up. One of the security guys had stepped up to her car to say he was sorry, but she was too late, and told her she'd missed a great party.

The man was a damned giant. *Good choice for a bouncer, brothers mine!* She'd given him a disappointed smile, thanked him, put her rental back into gear, and headed to her family's home. Cash had been updating her on the renovations and additions they'd made, but the scope of the changes had still taken her breath away as she'd pulled up in front of the house. *Yep, it's official. Collin has more money than God.*

The additions on both ends of the house were enormous, and the rock porch and the landscaping and—well, hell, the list was endless. Geez, she could hardly wait to snoop around in the morning. But right now, she was beyond exhausted. Just as she was pulling the last suitcase from the trunk, she noticed the truck she'd seen in the club's parking lot pull around the corner of the long drive.

She felt as if she'd stepped into a spotlight, but she hadn't moved. For just a second, she worried one of her crazy fans had followed her, then logic kicked in, and she knew there was no way anyone could have known her plans. Hell, she hadn't decided to come home until late last night. But still... the hair on the back of her neck stood up, and warning bells were ringing in her mind.

Shaking the feeling off, she watched as the truck turned back around and drove away. *Must have been one of my brothers' staff making sure I wasn't a criminal. Probably figured I'm safe, not many burglars park in front of their targets' home and unload five massive suitcases that are obviously already packed to near bursting.*

Cripes, she was starting to get punchy. Making jokes in her mind and laughing out loud at her own silliness was a sure sign she was beyond exhausted. Just as she unlocked the front door, she heard a woman scream. It took a few seconds for the logical side of her brain to take the reins from the fight-or-flight side, but when it did, she recognized the sound for what it was. Yes, indeed, this is what she got for not letting the Terrifying Three, as she often referred to her brothers, know she was on her way home.

Making her way down the long hallway to the opposite wing of the house, she easily found the apartment Cash told her had been added. *Damn, sometimes it's great having a super-wealthy brother.* The space was almost double the size of her apartment in New York and much more elegant. Even though the agency she'd worked for had done a great job making sure she'd had the highest-paying jobs, she'd been conservative with her spending. Truthfully, it had seemed ridiculous to pay an exorbitant amount of money for an apartment she wasn't home enough to enjoy.

Maneuvering her suitcases down the long hall, looking for the bedroom, she was thrilled when she poked her head into the office they'd designed. She loved the wall of windows and knew they would give her a stunning view of the valley below. She could barely contain her excitement as she thought about the plans she had for her first clients. She was going to spend a few days resting, then she was going to throw herself into building a new career, and if no one ever took her damned picture again, it would suit her just fine.

NOAH DRUMMOND HAD gone to the Grand Opening of Red Clouds Dancing for one reason and one reason only—to see Ilaina Red Cloud. He'd worried his information had been wrong when her brothers whisked the blonde bombshell—they were all obviously interested in—out well before closing. Noah had been certain the brothers wouldn't have left if they'd known their sister was on her way home, but he'd stuck around until the bitter end, just in case.

He'd been sitting in his truck, letting it warm up when he noticed what he knew was a rental car pull up. Noah watched as the most beautiful woman in the entire world rolled down her window and spoke with the brute her brothers had hired as a bouncer. How the man hadn't recognized one of the most photographed women on the planet was a mystery for the ages, but it had been obvious when he'd watched in confusion as she'd driven off and headed down the private drive leading to her family's home.

Noah had followed to make sure she made it safely—he'd waited years for the chance to reclaim her and wasn't taking any chances now that he was so close to his goal. He'd seen her brothers' reactions when they'd seen him leaning against the bar, and he owed Alex Lamont for staying them. Noah's reputation as a playboy photographer wasn't even close to who he really was, but it had made a damned fine cover for the past several years, so he'd never made any attempt to set the record straight. Alex and Zach Lamont were among the few people locally who had any idea how much broader his job description had actually been.

Once he'd seen that Ilaina was safely parked in front of her home, he'd turned around and returned to his studio and loft. The renovations to the old mill were nearly complete, and he was thrilled with how it was coming together. The place had been nearly perfect for his needs, and he'd been grateful to Zach for suggesting it. Noah loved the huge windows, large open spaces, and the place had a view of the mountains that always took his breath away.

He was proud of everything he'd accomplished in the past few months, and for the first time, he'd actually been grateful for the ridiculous sums of money the United States military had been willing to pay him for his assistance. He still laughed about that expression—but then "assistance" looked a lot better on the certificate they'd given him than the truth, that was for sure.

Walking up the floating staircase, he thought about the elusive woman most of the world knew only as Ilaina. For years, he'd kept his distance, not wanting to put her on the radar of anyone he worked with or for. Knowing who a person loved gave friends and enemies alike too much leverage. But now that he was retired, all bets were off. Stopping in his living room to look at the best picture he'd ever taken, he couldn't help touching the canvas. Once, a long time ago—long before she'd become famous—she'd let him take her picture, and it was still the most beautiful photo he'd ever taken. It was also the best picture he'd ever seen of her. It had been just minutes after he'd made love to her, and somehow, the camera had caught every nuance of her in the soft afterglow of that intimate moment. The effect was one of pure enchantment.

Very soon, my beautiful Ilaina, very soon I'm going to make you understand why I left.

Chapter 10

LAYLA WOKE UP surrounded by warm skin, and even in the dark room, she had no trouble telling Cash was on her right, and Clay was snuggled against her left side. She wondered where Collin was until she felt him shift and realized the weight that had been over her calves had been lifted. She basked in the feeling of them all around her until she realized what had awakened her—she had to use the restroom.

She started trying to free herself from Clay's hold, and when he mumbled and tightened his arm around her, she whispered she'd be back in just a bit. He reluctantly lifted her over his body and set her gently on the floor.

"Hurry back, baby, I don't want to sleep with my brothers without you between us." He gave her a small smile, then fell back to sleep before she'd even turned to make her way to the bathroom.

After leaving the bathroom, Layla put on the silk robe she'd worn earlier and made her way down the hall, intending to find the kitchen and get a glass of water. As she rounded the corner into what turned out to be a huge kitchen, she saw the most beautiful woman she'd ever seen standing at the large island in the center of the room. Both women screamed in surprise before the dark-haired beauty started waving her hands and shushing her, all the while darting glances up the hall where the men slept.

Layla's breathing finally calmed down, and only then did she realize that the woman standing barefoot in faded jeans and a cut off T-shirt with "Runways aren't just for planes" across the front was none other than supermodel Ilaina.

"Hell's bells and hand grenades, you scared the shit out of me." It took a few seconds before Layla's brain fully engaged, so she simply stood stock-still, staring at one of the most famous faces in the world.

"You must be Layla. Cash has told me so much about you. You are every bit as beautiful as he described you." Extending her hand, she said, "I'm Ilaina Red Cloud, I'm so sorry I scared you. I tried to get here in time for the Grand Opening, but things didn't work out the way I'd planned."

Layla tried to smile, but she was still too stunned to do much more than stare. Her shock must have shown because Ilaina looked at her and shook her head.

"Honey, you better have a seat, you look a bit—" Her words were cut off as her three brothers skidded around the corner in nothing but their jeans.

Ilaina looked up and smiled. "Hey, you guys, have a little respect, here. Didn't your mama teach you it's not proper to come into the kitchen without a shirt on? And nobody wants to see your big ole bare boy feet. Hell, boys have hair on their toes, that's just too gross for words. And the whole effect is just way more visual information than I ever want of you three stooges." With those words, she launched herself into Cash's waiting arms. Layla didn't doubt for a minute she and Ilaina Red Cloud were going to be great friends. She loved the way the woman held her own and thought on her feet. *Oh, Tori and the girls are going to love her too!*

Watching as Cash crushed his sister in a hug, Layla was touched by the obvious affection the two shared. Ilaina hugged each of her brothers, but her face clearly reflected her deep love and a special level of respect that seemed to be reserved for Cash. When they'd all exchanged greetings and promised to meet back in the kitchen in a few hours for a "real Red Cloud breakfast," whatever that meant, the men led her back down the hallway to the bedroom.

Just as they settled her back into the massive bed, she muttered she had never gotten the glass of water she'd gone downstairs for. Clay reached over and handed her a small glass of water she hadn't even noticed him carrying back to the room.

She downed the entire glass before handing it back to him with a shy smile of thanks. The last thing she remembered was Cash's soft chuckle behind her before he pulled her tight against his warm chest and spoke against her ear.

"Love, you took five years off my life. Hell, we were all halfway down the hall in our fucking birthday suits before we heard Lainy's voice and had to come back to get our jeans."

Layla remembered smiling, then she just slid back to sleep.

NICK LANG PACED the small holding cell like the caged animal he was. Just a few more hours, and he'd be out of this fucking hell-hole forever. It had taken years, but he'd finally won his case on appeal. What monkey-run court took the testimony of a damned teenage girl over all the witnesses he'd managed to "find" anyway?

It hadn't mattered how much pressure he'd put on his niece or her worthless mother, the bitch had still testified. At least his sister had kicked her out of the house, so he was sure she would be easy to eliminate. Hell, nobody cared when some streetwalker turned up dead in an alley. *God knows she'll be easy to find with that damned white-blonde hair of hers.*

One of his contacts in Colorado had let him know he'd seen her just a few days ago. The kid was obviously looking to move up quickly, and Nick would reward his loyalty so others would understand what it took to shine in the boss' eyes. He still didn't know why she was in Colorado, probably followed some sugar daddy.

Nick would spend a couple of days getting things together here, then head north and take care of her once and for all. Thinking about his niece always gave him a fucking migraine because the whole thing was such a fucked-up mess.

Jesus, the kid had been a dead ringer for Marilyn Monroe from the time she was twelve. He'd enjoyed taking her places back then. She'd been a great distraction while he'd done "business." If a cop happened by, he was always so distracted by Little Miss Perky and Blonde, he was oblivious to whatever Nick was up to.

The guard walked by for the fourth time in twenty minutes and glared at him. "Sit your ass down, Lang, we'll get to you soon enough. Getting sprung on a fucking technicality doesn't mean anybody in the front office thinks they need to bust their ass to speed up your paperwork."

Every guard in the damned place had been even nastier after Nick won his case. Oh sure, there had been several who had been willing to keep the perks coming his way for the right amount of money, but most of them had decided he was about a thousand feet below pond scum.

In a couple of hours, this place would be nothing but a nasty memory, and the opinions of the pencil dicks who'd held it over him for the past several years wouldn't mean squat. He'd be out of here and back on the street, making some serious cash in no time, and when he caught up with Layla, he intended to make her understand the importance of loyalty, right before he slit her fucking throat. Oh yeah, that was definitely going to send a strong message to the rest of his *family*. They'd give him the respect he deserved because he planned to leave no doubt they either backed him one hundred percent, or they were his enemy—there was nothing in between. They would know if he killed his own blood, he'd damned well kill any of them.

Chapter 11

L AYLA COULDN'T REMEMBER the last time she'd had so much fun at a meal. The Red Cloud siblings had worked together in the kitchen like a well-oiled machine despite their constant bickering and teasing banter. It was obvious their parents had made sure each of their sons learned to cook, and she would be sure and thank them for that when she met them because Lord love a leper, she could barely boil water without setting off the smoke detectors. Each of her tiny apartments over the years had been filled with smoke every time she'd decided cooking really couldn't be that hard, and she made another attempt. Finally, her last landlord had threatened to move her out onto the street if she didn't stop trying to "torch the place."

This morning, she'd opted to set the table and make toast and been thrilled when they hadn't turned into charred cinders. When Cash had noticed her beaming at the tall stack of golden brown bread slices, he'd raised an eyebrow in question. She'd excitedly told him she'd made the whole stack without the smoke alarms going off, and he should probably note it on the calendar for later submission to the history book people.

Cash had given her a bear hug and whispered in her ear that cooking wasn't even close to what he thought she did best. Layla knew her face had turned five shades of red when everyone else in the room burst out laughing.

She enjoyed watching the siblings as they spent most of the day catching up on each other's lives. Ilaina had made it clear to her brothers she loved the changes they'd made to their childhood home. When they'd gone downstairs, Layla had been delighted to see the basement was a walk-out, and their patio had a beautiful fire pit and an outdoor kitchen designed for entertaining large groups of friends.

When they'd entered what they called Layla's Beach, she had been completely overcome with emotion. Collin explained not long after they'd met in Houston, she had mentioned being worried about living in Colorado during the winter because she so loved the warmer temperatures of southern Texas. She remembered the conversation, it had been during their long drive north to her new home, and he'd been describing the beauty of snow glistening atop the tall pine trees. She'd shivered from head to toe before she explained her worries.

"Frack, I get all sad and sleepy if it's cloudy for more than a couple of days. What am I going to do when it's cloudy for days on end, and it's too cold to go outside and bask in the warm sun and recharge?"

When Collin led her into the Beach Room, she cried because his thoughtfulness touched her so. But then she squealed and kicked off her shoes before heading for the "sanded beach" that came complete with a tiki bar and beach chairs. Collin had shown her the lights and explained they were designed to imitate the day spectrum rays of the sun and were supposed to greatly alleviate symptoms of Seasonal Affective Disorder.

The large walk-in pool featured a small waterfall that was supposed to keep the oxygen level of the water at "optimum levels for various beneficial health effects." Clay had leaned close and whispered all that meant was that it was going to send bubbles dancing over every inch of her, and since they were going to make her swim "nekkid," those bubbles were going to dance over her clit and make her want them all the more.

Layla had been thinking about all the orgasms she had last night and quickly found herself fighting the heavy feeling of neediness in her lower abdomen and the throbbing in her clit when she felt Cash step up behind her and press his hard cock against her ass. That small move sent a bolt of electrified need shooting directly into her pussy.

She felt a flood of moisture coat her labia and begin trailing down the inside of her thighs. They showed her the swimsuits they purchased for her, then let her sit in the hot tub with Ilaina. But when Collin had helped her into one of his button-down shirts after he'd dried her, he'd very subtly taken her bottoms, so she'd spent the last hour sitting on a leather stool in front of the tiki bar with her very bare pussy moving over the rough texture of the leather. There had been several times she had nearly moaned out loud, and by the time Ilaina had gone upstairs, Layla was nearly ready to plunge her fingers deep and bring herself some relief.

Layla noticed they'd walked by one door that appeared heavier than the rest, and since the men hadn't made any effort to explain what the room held, she hadn't felt comfortable enough to ask. Ilaina had said her goodbyes late in the afternoon, citing fatigue and her body still adjusting to the time change. As soon as the men had known their sister was safely upstairs, Layla noticed a distinct change in the energy in the room.

WHEN LAYLA HAD hugged him after they'd shown her the beach room, all Collin could think about was stripping her and sinking as deep inside her as he could get. He'd had to endure a hard-on from hell most of the day and knew full well the only cure was going to be a naked sub with a couple of nice pink ass cheeks, and his cock pushed balls deep in her ass. Shaking off his dark thoughts, Collin turned to his younger brother.

"Clay, we're going to play with our sub. If you want to play, you are welcome to stay, but if you're going to squeak about what happens, head on upstairs." Collin saw Layla flush with arousal and could smell her honeyed pussy from where he was standing. When Clay stood exactly where he was and merely crossed his arms over his chest, Collin nodded, then turned to Layla.

"Come to me, sweetness."

He could tell her feet had started moving before her mind had even processed the words, and when she stood in front of him, he looked down and smiled.

"Such a good girl. Now, I want you to turn around and bend over the bar stool you have marked with your sweet arousal. Bend over and spread your legs." When she was in position, he pulled up the tail of the shirt she was wearing, exposing her bare ass.

He had to take a deep breath to stem his desire to paddle her just because he wanted to so badly. He ran his fingers through her wet folds, deliberately avoiding the one spot he knew would set her off, making her even wetter and causing her to begin moving. Collin wanted her body to crave their touch and the relief only they could provide. When Collin looked up, Clay was standing to the side with a look of complete awe.

"We are going to begin as we intend to go, sweetness. That means we will be playing with you in ways you have yet to even imagine, but there are rules as well. There will be times when we just want to look or touch you for no other purpose than it is what we desire. And you'll allow that because you'll know how much it pleases us."

He was running his hands over the smooth globes of her ass, his touch little more than a feather-light caress. She was already beginning to lose her ability to focus on his words which was exactly what he wanted. The goose-bumps spreading over her skin told him she was ready for more.

"None of us are big fans of panties. They are a nuisance if you ask me, so we don't want you to wear them when you're in this house."

Collin knew he was forcing Layla to split her concentration between futile attempts to process the sensations of pleasure flooding her and her mind's attempt to process the words he was speaking—that was on purpose and by design.

"The door down the hall you wondered about but were too polite to inquire about earlier? Panties are never allowed in that room—as a matter of fact, you will not be permitted to wear anything we haven't specifically asked you to wear when you are in there." He laughed at her startled gasp.

"Oh, my sweet, you are so very easy to read. You're an open book, and it's a part of your charm. It calls to the Dom in both Cash and me in ways we'd love to spend the rest of our lives showing you." Collin glanced up at Clay and smiled.

"Clay is a Dom, too—he just hasn't realized it yet. Oh, he may gain your submission through charm and subtle manipulation, but never doubt he gains your compliance even when you don't realize it is happening."

Collin watched as Clay's lips twitched, and Layla's eyes went wide. He applied a bit more pressure with his touch and was pleased to see her react immediately.

"Now, we'd like to know what exactly you had in mind when you thought about applying for membership to The ShadowDance Club."

"What? How?"

He knew he'd shocked her and keeping her off balance was all part of their plan. When she tried to stand up, Cash placed his hand between her shoulder blades and held her in place. Her frantic attempts to turn to her right were met with an even firmer hold, and Collin knew she hadn't realized Cash had moved to stand alongside her.

Collin watched as Cash leaned down and brushed her hair aside, then bit lightly on the nape of her neck. Her groaned response went straight to Collin's already throbbing cock. Cash spoke quietly, but he'd also made sure there was enough steel in his voice Layla wouldn't misunderstand his intent.

"Don't ever think you can keep a secret, love. We won't allow it, and every Dom in our group of friends will work with us to keep you safe."

Collin saw that she was confused by Cash's reference to her safety by the look on her face. She hadn't yet noticed the mirrors in the room, and that oversight was working to their advantage. They could see her expressions without her realizing she was being watched so closely, and that visual information was valuable indeed.

"Your safety involves everything from the deplorable vehicle you are driving to the small apartment you looked at in town last week." She gasped, and Collin watched in amusement as she stiffened in defiance. "You shouldn't be surprised we know about your apartment search, and I assure you the Lamonts are none too pleased to know you would prefer living in squalor with a damned propane wall unit that was built when Truman was President rather than continuing to enjoy their hospitality." Leaning down, so his face was mere inches from hers, Collin frowned.

"But you decided to expose yourself to all the potential risks of being an uncollared sub in a BDSM club. That reckless behavior added to the enormous risk you took last night by shoving your sweet ass back on my cock before I felt you were properly prepared. Those two offenses will be the main points we'll focus our attention on right now."

When he saw her expression harden, he pulled his hand from her and gave her a resounding swat. It hadn't been particularly hard, but it would have certainly gotten her attention.

"Be careful with your body language, sweetheart. We'll read you like a book and act accordingly."

Collin watched her breathing hitch, and when he glanced at Clay, he saw his brother's eyes were wide with desire. *Oh yeah, little brother, you're starting to understand the appeal, aren't you?* Returning his attention to the woman bent over in front of him he continued.

"You've done some reading about Dominant and submissive relationships, isn't that right, sweetness?" She nodded her head, and for now, that would be enough. "You've also spoken with Victoria and Katarina about their experiences?"

He wasn't surprised she was hesitant to answer. Until

she was truly a part of the lifestyle, she wouldn't realize answering questions such as the ones he planned to ask would not be considered a breach of trust or confidentiality by her friends.

"Love," Cash assured, "you are not betraying your friends by answering our questions, and you'll learn more about that as we go along. But for now, you'll just have to trust I will never lie to you. The bottom line question is— you are aware you are a submissive, correct?"

She nodded once, but Collin was sure the motion had been so automatic, it occurred without her mind ever processing the question. Looking up at Cash, Collin couldn't hold back his smile. Even though they hadn't shared a woman or played together in years, they were obviously still very much in sync.

Cash leaned down and ran his tongue from the base of her neck to the sensitive spot just above her ass. Layla arched her back into the touch and moaned. Cash kissed both dented spots above her ass that were now much too pronounced since she'd lost weight.

"Do you have any idea how much we want you? How much we adore you? How very perfect you are for each of us? Your submission is a gift given from the heart and soul of a strong woman, and we'll treasure it and treat it with the love and care it deserves. Hold those words in your heart, my love."

Collin stepped closer and pressed his jean-clad erection against her bare ass.

"You'll go to The Club when we decide you are ready and not before, sweetness. Right now, it would not be in your best interest for several reasons. The biggest concern is that you don't know all the rules, and that could easily get you into a situation we wouldn't be able to do much to help with. And quite frankly, the idea of another man having the opportunity to punish you is enough to give me nightmares." He stepped back again and started gently squeezing her ass cheeks.

"This body belongs to the three of us, pet. No one else touches it without our express permission, and just so you know, we only share with each other. We're going to show you what's behind that door." He ran his fingers through the swollen folds of her pussy lips, pleased to find she was soaking wet. Now, he only hoped she stayed that way after she got a look at their playroom.

Chapter 12

C LAY HAD NEVER been so turned on in his entire life. He was starting to understand why his fathers, brothers, and friends raved about the benefits of a D/s lifestyle. Not that any of them were interested in a twenty-four-seven arrangement, but it was easy to see how beautifully Layla responded, and that alone was enough to sell him on the idea. Before they left the beach room, he pulled her against his chest.

"Baby, you are so fucking amazing. Your body responds in ways we could have only ever dreamed of finding in a woman. Before we leave this room, I just want to make sure you know how very proud I am of you." When he released her and looked down into the face he knew God had modeled after an angel. He was humbled by the trust he saw reflected in her sparkling emerald eyes.

"That is probably the nicest thing anyone has ever said to me."

He watched as she took several deep breaths to regain her composure and wondered how difficult her life must have been for those simple words to have made such an impact.

"I honestly don't remember the last time anyone told me they were proud of me before you and your brothers. I know they are simple words for you because you grew up with a family who understood their importance, but my family didn't see... well, let's just say they didn't see that I had much value as anything but a distraction."

Clay thought his heart would break in two at her words, and it took him a few seconds to regain focus. When she leaned forward and put her forehead against his chest and whispered, "Thank you," he couldn't help but pick her up and pull her tight against his chest. This time, she wrapped her legs around his waist, and the heat of her bare sex sent his blood rushing south in a big way. When they reached the playroom's locked door, he set her back on her feet.

"Down you go, baby. You need to pay very close attention to the rules." He turned her toward Cash, then stepped aside. He listened as Cash told her she would not be permitted to wear anything inside the playroom unless one of them had given it to her for that purpose. Her eyes opened wide when she realized she would be naked while they would not—well, at least not in the beginning.

Collin had already stepped into the playroom to set things up, and Layla stood facing the two of them outside the door. Cash brushed the pads of his fingers along the underside of her jaw and nodded when she met his gaze.

"Tonight, we aren't going to use any strict protocol, so you are welcome to ask us anything as long as you are respectful. If you get snarky, love, you will be punished. We'll also insist you have a safe word. Do you know what that is?"

Clay watched as she slowly nodded her head, and Cash pulled her hand to his mouth, turned it, and so he could press a lingering kiss in the center of her palm.

"Love, anytime we are in a scene or even preparing for a scene, you will be required to give your answers with words—nods or shakes of your head will not be good enough. We don't want there to be any questions or mistakes in our communication, do you understand? Also, you'll use formal titles with your answers, for example, 'Yes, Sir' or 'Yes, Master' once you are more comfortable with that title. And yes, my love, I saw your reaction to the word. Have you heard the way Tori addresses Trace on occasion?" Cash and Clay both laughed out loud at her wide-eyed look.

"Yes, I see that it just clicked into place for you, didn't it? Damn, you are so amazing, and your genuine reactions bring me more joy than I can even begin to tell you." Cash leaned forward and kissed her forehead. "We'll be forever in Tori's debt for recommending you to the Lamonts."

Clay ran his hands over her shoulders and squeezed to let her know he was still right behind her, giving his brother a few seconds to bring the emotion Clay saw in his dark eyes under control. Giving the tight muscles a firm press of his thumbs, Clay was rewarded with her soft moan of pleasure.

Cash chuckled at her reaction. "Love, a safe word?"

"Yes, Ca… I mean, yes, Sir. I know what a safe word is. When I moved here and found out about The Club, I started doing some reading online in my spare time. I'd like to use the stoplight system The ShadowDance Club uses if that's okay, that way… well, when you all take me there, I'll feel like I fit in better."

"Good enough," Cash smiled and nodded. "Now, strip, love."

Clay watched as Cash took a step back, so the two of them were standing shoulder to shoulder. At that moment, Clay realized their stances were nearly mirror images— arms crossed over their chests, their legs shoulder width apart.

Oh yeah, a definite sign there. Fuck me, I'm more like my big brothers than I realized. Christ, I can smell her arousal, and it's going to make me blow like a fucking teenager if we don't get her inside the playroom so we can fuck her—Now!

WHEN CASH HAD told her to strip, Layla had been shocked to see little black dots in her vision and worried for several seconds she was going to pass out. Even though he didn't move closer to touch her, he did notice.

"Layla, take a breath, right now."

The commanding tone of his voice was all it took to startle her back to the moment, and she gulped in a huge breath of air. Shit, she hadn't even realized she'd been holding her breath. Why was she worried about stripping when she hadn't been intimidated before about them seeing her body? What possible reason could she have for denying them now? *Maybe because you've been ordered to remove the clothing yourself.*

Damn it… she *had* been planning to apply to The Club because the more Tori and Kat had talked, the more interested she'd become. Everything she'd read had told her that her friends were right, she was a sub to the bone. Oh sure, she was a wiseass and braver than she was smart sometimes, but there wasn't anything in the entire world she wanted more than to please the people she cared about.

Hell, that was a large part of the reason she'd been so devastated when she'd had to testify against her Uncle Nick. And when her entire family had turned on her, it had nearly broken her.

"Layla, I don't know where you have gone, but I don't like seeing that sadness in your eyes. Come back to me, love."

She refocused on his face and was mortified knowing she'd totally spaced out. Blinking quickly to push back the tears filling her eyes, Layla made a sincere effort to smile up at his compassion-filled expression. She muttered a quick apology and quickly stripped off the shirt and her bikini top. Folding them hurriedly, she handed them to Cash.

"Such a good girl. We'll be discussing where you went later, love. I want to know what could have caused that forlorn expression. Whoever is responsible for that is going to be answering to the three of us."

She could tell he was dead serious, and her heart swelled with love for the three men who seemed to want her, dents and all. Layla knew she couldn't think about forever because she'd have to disappear once her uncle was released, but she could certainly enjoy her time with them now.

Walking through the door into what both Cash and Collin had referred to as their playroom seemed like she'd stepped back in time and straight into a Middle Ages torture chamber. *Holy fucking fantasy-land, I think I have made a really big mistake here. This is way over my head. And what in the holy hell is that table for? I don't want a doctor to come in here. I hate those exams, they are too... Oh, God, I'm not ready for this... I have to get out of here... oh, shit... oh—*

Cash must have noticed her panic because gave her a sharp swat to her bare ass. When she was finally able to focus her attention on him, he was shaking his head.

"Love, you were speaking each of those thoughts out

loud, did you know that?" He laughed, then continued, not bothering to wait for her answer. "No, I can see by your expression you did not realize you were narrating everything going through your mind. So, let's address those *things*, shall we? We call it a playroom because we 'play' with you in here. And before you ask—no. No other woman has ever been in this room. This room was merely a dream until we met you. It is not a torture chamber— well, not unless you're naughty, then... maybe."

She had started looking around again and could feel her breathing starting to speed up, and those fucking black dots were back. *Damn, I hate those fucking dots. And I'm cold. And the top of my head feels all tingly. And what if I hate this? What if they kick me to the curb, and I have to see them with someone else? Shit, the dots are getting bigger.*

Layla felt like someone had set her ass on fire. No sooner had the thought moved through her mind, she realized Collin was standing in front of her with his hands on her shoulders. He all but shouted something, but she couldn't hear over the roar of the blood rushing through her ears. *Damn, lightning just struck my ass again. How was that possible in the basement, anyway?*

When Collin crushed his mouth to hers, she finally felt like she'd come back to the moment. He'd pulled her against his chest, his hands moving in soothing circles over her bare back, and for some odd reason, those circles were the most soothing feeling in the world at this moment. His kiss was more of a claiming than seduction, and she knew he was using it to distract her from her panic. She wanted to show him how grateful she was, so she pressed herself into his chest. She was determined to keep her head above water when he finally pulled back and brushed his thumbs over her cheeks.

"Better?"

When she just nodded, he raised a brow and waited.

"Yes, sir. Thank you… for, well… for bringing me back… I really hate those dots."

She wasn't sure what she'd expected, but his bark of laughter certainly wouldn't have made her list of *possibles* that's for sure. She stiffened her spine and met his gaze, hoping he'd understand she was ready to try again. He obviously understood because he stepped back and smiled at her.

"You are so brave. I'm proud of you for pulling yourself back for us, and for the record, we don't want you to see those dots either. Not even when we're playing. If you see them again, we'll expect you to use your safe word. Now, I heard you tell your other two Masters you'll be using the stoplight safe words. That's a great choice because I think you'll be more likely to use yellow than a full-fledged safe word."

Layla wasn't sure how he'd known that, but she was sure he was right. "Can I ask a question, please?" She knew immediately what she'd done wrong when she saw his slight frown. "Oh, I mean, may I ask a question, please, Sir?" *Ahh, pay dirt. A smiling Dom is a good thing. I don't know much about this, but I do know that much.*

"Good save, sweetness, and yes, you may." Collin's smile warmed her, and she tried to focus on him and not worry about what Cash was doing. She was worried she'd offended him since he was no longer standing close to her.

"Don't worry about where your other Masters are, they have not left you. Now, what's your question?" Layla let out a relieved breath and nodded.

"Right… well, I read that some Doms are, well… done with a sub if he or she uses their safe word. Um… will you be…" She didn't finish the sentence because he'd stepped close again.

"No. We will not *be done* with you, not by any stretch of the imagination, sweetness. We *will* stop the scene immediately and provide aftercare for you. We'll wrap you in a blanket and get you something to drink. Once you're settled, we'll all sit down and talk about what happened, where it went wrong, and what we'll be able to do differently next time. We will be *done* for that day only.

"The only reason I say we'll be done for the day is because we'll want you to have a bit of time to process everything. Now, that being said, if we are doing our jobs right, you won't need your safe word because we'll be watching every nuance and reaction—basically, we'll be watching every breath you take. We want you to use the word yellow if you feel like you're getting overwhelmed. That word serves as a heads-up that we need to take a minute and reassess things. That is why I was glad to hear you'd chosen The Club's safe word system."

Layla felt as if someone had lifted a huge burden off her shoulders. She hadn't realized how worried she'd been about that part of a D/s scene. When she'd read that some Doms don't ever play with a sub again once she uses her safe word, she'd felt her heart sink at the thought of losing the three men she was already falling for in a big way. When she'd walked through the door of their playroom and seen everything, she'd panicked at the thought she was in so far over her head. Knowing she was, in no way, ready for this and at the same time being afraid she'd be too petrified of losing them to use her safe word had scared her to death. Cripes, if she didn't tell them she was terrified, she could get hurt… again. When Layla suddenly realized she'd been speaking out loud, she froze.

Chapter 13

COLLIN HAD NEVER been so swept away by the words from a sub in his entire life. When he glanced at his brothers, it was easy to see they felt the same way. The fact that she had been frightened they'd dump her if she used her safe word bothered him as a Dom.

God damn it, the internet was a great tool, but it also an open door for people who wanted nothing more than to prey on innocents like the beautiful woman in front of him. The worst part was she'd been carrying that burden around, and they hadn't known she was suffering. They'd been busy making sure Layla understood what the three of them expected from her, and none of them had taken time to assure the most important person in the equation it was going to be impossible for her to fail.

They had failed to make sure she understood what she could expect from each of them in return for the gift of her trust. He had been a Dom practically since he'd first become sexually active and had never made such a critical error—and to make it with the woman he wanted to build a future with shook him to his core.

Cash stepped up to Layla shaking his head. "Love, I am so, so sorry. If we had known this was worrying you, we could have taken that burden from you easily. I want you to make us all a promise—if you *ever* have a concern or a

110

question is weighing on your heart, I want you to swear you'll bring that concern to one or all of us immediately. One of the joys of a D/s relationship is that it is *supposed* to make your life easier. We want you to be able to let yourself go and be exactly who you are when you are with us. As your Doms, we should be carrying those burdens, not you, do you understand?"

"Yes, I think so, but... well, it's all very new, and I don't want to mess up because—" She'd stopped speaking and was biting her lower lip, and Collin could see she was trying to find the right words. None of them spoke, they simply waited for her to pull her thoughts together. "Well, let's just say, once a long time ago, I did something I knew then and still believe was the right thing to do, and even though I did what was right, I still lost everything... my family, my home... So, I'm a bit gun-shy, you know?"

Cash nodded once before kissing her forehead. "We're going to ask you more about that later, but for now, I just want you to make that promise, love. Promise us you will bring your burdens and worries to us so we can help even if it's only to act as your sounding board. As soon as we hear those words, I think it's time for some pleasure."

Layla seemed to understand it was important to each of the men because she looked at each of them and promised to bring her concerns to them in the future rather than holding them in.

Collin breathed out a sigh of relief and stepped forward. "Thank you for that show of trust, sweetness. Now, let's play." He smiled at her, and his heart nearly melted when he saw her tiny shoulders relax, her relief evident in every bit of her body language. He led her over to a long narrow table he knew had reminded her of the ones found in doctors' offices.

"Up you go. We're going to do a little sensation play—don't bite your lip, sweetheart, you're going to love this, I promise."

He watched her closely for any signs of hesitance or apprehension while they secured her to the table, but Collin saw nothing but signs of arousal—her pulse had quickened, and her eyes were so dilated, there was only a narrow ring of their lovely emerald green visible now.

Moving to the head of the table, Collin took a black silk scarf from his back pocket. Her eyes went impossibly wide when she saw what he was holding, and he couldn't help but smile. *Fuck me, I can already smell the sweet cream her body is using to coat those lovely pussy lips in anticipation of our possession.*

"You are so beautiful, all laid out for our pleasure. We're taking away your sense of sight so you'll concentrate on all the sensations you're experiencing rather than what you're seeing. Really bright women are so keenly aware of their surroundings, they tend to assess visually at alarmingly rapid rates which requires so much of their attention, they miss a lot of the pleasure."

He trailed the black silk down one side of her upper torso before circling it around her navel and moving up the opposite side.

"Let us be responsible for your pleasure, Layla. If you don't have to process visual information, it will make it much easier for you to enjoy the sensations." He leaned forward and kissed each of her eyelids closed. "Such a sweet subbie—so trusting and perfect." He tied the scarf securely over her eyes and smiled when she shuddered.

Collin ran a finger down the side of her face and continued down until he was circling one of her pink nipples. The sweet peak of her breast drew up tightly, and she gasped and moaned as the flush of pleasure began spreading over her chest.

"You are so responsive. Do you know what a turn-on it is to see you respond to our touch like this? Most people don't think about the how much Doms value their sub's trust and how honored they are to provide their pleasure." He leaned down and circled her nipple with the tip of his tongue, then blew a small puff of air over the damp skin. Watching as she tried to arch her back, he chuckled. "Your body is chasing the feelings now that your mind has let go. Perfect."

Cash handed a feather to Clay, and Collin saw him directing their youngest brother to draw the feather lightly up and down the insides of Layla's thighs. When Clay started the tantalizing tease, Cash reached under the table and hit the control that slowly moved the two parts of the table apart until her thighs were spread wide. Cash handed a small pussy flogger to Collin, then moved to the side to ready his part of the scene.

Collin watched as Clay drew sensual patterns up and back down the tender skin on the insides of Layla's legs. He caught on quickly as Collin had known he would. Clay was varying not only the pressure but keeping the patterns random, so she was never sure where the feather was going to trail next.

Collin pointed out her shallow breaths, so Clay knew this was exactly where they wanted her to be. When he gave his youngest brother a quick signal to wind down, Collin watched as Clay danced the feather over her ivory-skinned perfection until he was able to speak into her ear.

"You are amazing, baby. Watching your body respond to one of the most important symbols of my ancestors was one of the most erotic things I have ever seen. You are perfect." Clay gave her a quick kiss before stepping back.

Standing between Layla's splayed legs, Collin lightly trailed the soft deerskin strips of the flogger over her belly and smiled when goosebumps raced over her entire body. He deliberately used his Dom voice when he spoke to her this time. It was time for her to start learning there were all sorts of clues when they were playing. It wouldn't be long before just using a certain tone of voice would be enough to make her pussy flood with moisture and anticipation.

"My lovely sub, I'm going to be introducing you to a flogger." He saw her muscles tense but didn't stop speaking. "Floggers serve many purposes, but I'll use them today with one goal in mind. I want to bring more blood to the surface of your skin because the effect is a heightened level of sensitivity. That increased perception will set the stage for what Cash is planning. You see, my sweet pet, each of us has particular skills and preferences and are going to enjoy finding out how each adds to your pleasure."

Collin started flicking the strands of the flogger lightly over her lower abdomen with just enough force to give her a light tickling sensation. While he spread out the soft thudding of the leather strips over her torso, Cash started lowering the canvas from the ceiling. Collin saw Clay's eyes widen, but he had to give his younger brother credit, the youngest Red Cloud brother didn't speak the questions that were so clearly written in his eyes. Collin gave a short nod to let his brother know they were on track and returned his attention to Layla.

"We have something special for you, and I want you to answer my next question with just two words, sweet pet. Your answer is either 'Yes, sir' or 'No, sir'—okay, here we go. Do you trust we'll never harm you?" He was surprised to discover he was more nervous about her answer than he thought he'd be. He'd never really cared about a sub's answer before, but with this woman, having her in the right frame of mind and lost in pleasure was the most important thing in the world.

Her answer was a breathy whispered, "Yes, sir."

"Thank you, pet. Now, you're going to feel a piece of canvas come down over you. You're going to notice two things. First, your face will not be covered, and second, as soon as it touches you, you'll be secured to it by the Velcro bands on the outsides of the bindings holding you to this table. We'll use the canvas to rotate you slowly until you are face down, then we'll be able to proceed."

They wouldn't often tell her what was coming, but he didn't want her anxious or frightened since this was her first experience with play involving equipment. He'd filled the room with all sorts of wonderful surprises he could hardly wait to show her, so he wanted to make sure she enjoyed her first exposure to true D/s play.

Once they had her flipped over and the thin top of the table moved out of the way, he resumed lightly flogging her back, moving in a slow pattern from her shoulders to her ass. Damn, he could hardly wait until he could tie her to a St. Andrew's cross and flog her into sub-space.

She was already panting with a need so intense, he was sure she wouldn't have even been able to speak. He leaned over and ran his fingers down her slit and circled her opening twice before pushing his fingers into her. Her vaginal walls tightened on his fingers as if they were trying to pull him deeper, and he could feel her muscles starting to quiver with an impending orgasm, so he withdrew his fingers.

"Oh no you don't, my pet, you do not have permission to come yet." Now that she was on the canvas, her position was easy to manipulate, and he used the foot pedals to lower her head and knees just a bit, so her lovely ass was peaked. Taking the bullet vibrator he'd set nearby, he slid it into her, then pushed another into her sweet ass. Before he moved back, he leaned forward and kissed each of her ass cheeks.

"Get ready to fly, pet."

CASH HAD BEEN standing back, watching Collin flog the woman who was already becoming the center of their family. Her pulse rate had kicked up, and her breathing was becoming shallow and rapid—perfect. He rolled the cart holding his supplies close and knew the minute she'd heard the noise. Leaning down, he brushed her hair off to the side and secured it with a clip.

"I'm going to be using low temp candles, love. This is a very intense experience, and I don't want either of us getting so caught up in it, we get wax in your beautiful hair." He'd felt her tense when he'd said their word *wax*, but he continued. "Do you want to use your safe word, love?" He waited, already convinced he knew the answer, but he'd wait patiently, anyway.

"No, Sir. But I appreciate it when you talk to me because that way I feel connected... I'm not scared then." Her words were music to his ears. To have her place her trust in him was a precious gift. All she'd asked in return was he keep her connected through his voice. She humbled him.

"You please me in ways I don't even know words to describe, my love. I will be happy to talk to you as we enjoy this together. But… if I do everything right, you'll be past listening very soon, so don't try to hold on to the words. When you have the chance to jump off into the happy place, take it, love, because that is exactly where I'm taking you."

He didn't expect a response, so he just picked up the first candle and tested the temperature by dribbling wax over his inner arm from various distances until he knew exactly how far he wanted to be from his sub's lovely back.

"As I said, these candles have very low melting temperatures, so when the wax touches you, you're going to feel a flash of heat, then it will cool quickly, leaving you with another layer of the sensation memory we're building. Each splash of wax will add an additional layer to that memory until you are floating in a place of pure pleasure. I won't be talking as much as we proceed because I want to concentrate. Focus on how it feels, let those feelings paint a picture in your mind, just as I'm going to paint one over your exquisite back and perfect ass."

He'd no sooner spoken the last words than he began a diagonal line that started at her left shoulder and ended atop her right hip. She gasped as the first wax hit her sensitive skin, but by the time he'd finished the first pass, she was already moaning in pleasure. *Oh, my sweet Layla, you are so perfect. I want to send you straight into orgasmic bliss.*

Cash spent the next half hour drawing intricate patterns of wax and listening as Layla's responses became more slurred as she slipped over the line into what he'd heard other subs describe as *the zone*. Scientifically, it was better defined as an endorphin-induced state of euphoria, but it was most commonly known by Doms and subs alike as "sub-space."

Glancing up at Collin, he quickly gave him the signal

for five seconds, then he leaned close to her ear and commanded, "Come for me, love. Scream your pleasure for your Masters." At his words, Collin had hit the remotes for both vibes she'd no doubt forgotten were seated deep in her pussy and rear hole.

Her response was instant and probably pinged the Richter scale in three states. Her passionate scream echoed off the stone-covered playroom, and he was grateful they had the foresight to soundproof the room. They didn't need Ilaina breaking down the door to rescue her new friend. Cash silently wondered if Layla was going to be hoarse tomorrow, her scream had been so raw and sustained. Watching as she rode wave after wave of pleasure, he smiled when she finally sagged back against the canvas. She looked as if every muscle had finally let go from sheer sated exhaustion. As he lifted her from the canvas and made his way to the large bath at the back of the cavernous room, he noticed Clay hovering near his elbow.

"She's fine, little brother, she isn't fully back with us yet, but that is as it should be. We want to ease her back because it's an emotional roller coaster for a little while after such a strong climax. This is a critical bonding time between Doms and subs."

He had plenty of material for Clay to read. It would help his youngest brother understand the dynamics, both physical and psychological of power exchanges. From the expressions he saw pass over his youngest brother's face during the entire scene, Clay would devour the material.

Chapter 14

C ASH WASN'T SURE Layla would remember them
cleaning the wax from her body, holding her in the
warm bath, or massaging an aloe-based moisturizer into
her dewy skin. When he wrapped her in a soft blanket and
carried her back upstairs and into the living room, she'd
barely stirred.

He was lost in thought with her sitting cradled in his
lap and staring into the fire crackling in the fireplace when
he glanced down at her heart-shaped face, surprised to see
her looking at him. Her green eyes were bright with
curiosity, and he felt overwhelmed by the trust he saw
reflected in their green depths.

"Welcome back, love." He smiled at her and kissed the
tip of her nose.

"That was amazing. I don't have any words to describe
it." She looked around, and when she didn't see his brothers, she asked, "Where are Collin and Clay?" He saw the
self-doubt fill her eyes before her next words were even
spoken. "Did I do something wrong?"

"Absolutely not, in fact, you were perfect. My brothers
and I know in order for us to build the kind of life we want
with you, we'll need time alone as a couple. Remember,
we grew up with three fathers, so we're at an advantage
here. We've seen what a successful polyamorous marriage

looks like. We'll talk about this a lot because success is dependent upon clear and continuous open communication."

When he saw her start to chew on her bottom lip, he knew she was worried about being equitable with her time. His mother said this was an issue he needed to address early in their relationship. She explained how terrified she'd been, worrying she wouldn't remember whose turn it was to sleep where.

His mom told Cash she had even kept a secret chart until the dads had found it and explained it wasn't her job to keep everything straight. He spent several minutes recounting that conversation to Layla and was glad he had because her relief was easy to see.

"Love, there will be times when you want time alone, and we want you to feel free to express that need. Now, if we think you are trying to hide something, either physically or emotionally, we may not allow you to keep to yourself because anything that relates to your well-being is going to be discussed between all four of us. If you want to relax one evening or just need a night of cuddling, we'll expect you to be open and honest about those needs. Can you do that for us?"

Layla nodded her head and smiled shyly at him. "You know, I'll probably have all the alone time I'll need or want when I'm at my apartment. I've spent years alone, so I doubt it's going to be a problem."

"Well, we'll see how much time you spend there, shall we?" He chuckled at her confused look. "Love, we'll be using every trick at our disposal to keep you here as much as possible until we can convince you to *officially* move in. Remember, the suite at the end of the hall was designed and built for *you*. When we are not sleeping with you, we'll be in our own rooms."

Now that he knew she was fully engaged again, he wanted her with every fiber of his being. Lowering his lips to hers, Cash kissed her lightly at first, but when she started squirming on his cock, he knew it was time to move back to the bedroom. He'd like nothing more than to make sweet love to her here in front of the fire, but until his sister's routine was more established, that wouldn't be an option.

Without breaking the kiss, Cash made his way down the hall and into the bedroom before setting her on her feet beside the massive bed. He was grateful to whichever one of his brothers had turned down the bed for them and vowed to return that favor in the near future. When he saw uncertainty in her eyes, he asked, "What are you thinking about, love?"

"I was just wondering, do all the same rules apply when it's just the two of us? I don't want to mess up and get punished because I didn't know something I should have." He pulled her lower lip from between her teeth and kissed her gently.

"Love, you will never be punished for something you didn't know, and yes, the same rules will apply if we are in a scene, no matter if it is one, two, or all three of your Masters. With Collin, sex will probably always involve some level of D/s play. That isn't true with Clay nor will it always be true with me." He was pleased to see her relax, so he went on.

"Tonight is about me making love to the woman who has captured my heart. I want to feel your body wrap itself around me. I want to sink into your silky, wet heat and push my cock so deep, you won't know where I end and you begin."

While he'd been speaking he'd dropped the sweatpants he'd put on after his quick shower downstairs. He slowly opened the blanket he'd tucked around her and let it fall to the floor before moving them both to the bed.

"You are so very beautiful. The moment I walked into the lobby where you were working, I knew you belonged to me. I swear to you the whole world shifted on its axis at that moment."

He positioned himself between her thighs and began stringing small bites followed by soothing kisses down the side of her neck. When he reached the sensitive spot where the neck joins the shoulder, his bite was a bit stronger, and he savored the way she arched against his chest.

The needy little sounds she made went straight to his cock, and he relished the opportunity to move further down and suck on her sweet-tasting nipples. He loved how they beaded tightly against the roof of his mouth, their sweet taste a temptation he doubted he'd ever be able to resist. Kissing his way back up her neck, he spread her legs with his knees and spoke softly against the shell of her ear.

"Are you wet for me, my love? Are you ready for me to fill you with my aching cock? I need you. I need to feel your body pliant and yielding beneath me. Give yourself to me, love."

"Oh, yes, please... I need you, too." Those few words were all he needed to hear. He thrust his hips forward and seated himself fully in her wet silk.

Groaning at the feeling of her tight sheath, he relished the grip of delicate tissues still swollen from their earlier scene. He was so close to the edge, he worried it was going to be over much too soon. Cash would make sure she came again before he let go and took his pleasure in the deep strokes his body was craving, but her next words pushed his control right off his radar.

"Oh my God in heaven, you feel so good inside me. Nothing feels as good as this. Please, I need to feel your cock sliding in and out of me."

"Fuck!" The single word was all he could manage before he was pounding in so deep, he knew the tip of his cock was pressing against her cervix. He felt her shatter in his arms a split second before his world exploded in a whirling vortex of shimmering lights and pure spiritual sensuality. He would have sworn he'd seen a glimpse of heaven in those seconds. It was like being launched into the heavens and being surrounded by nothing but pure pleasure.

When their breathing started to return to normal, he rolled to the side, taking her with him. Wrapping his leg around her, he kept his cock buried inside her and pulled her tightly against his chest.

"I'm going to stay inside you, love. The warrior in me wants you to know you belong to me and that it is my seed filling your body. I look forward to the day when your sweet belly is round with our child. We'll fill this house with the love and laughter of a large family."

He worried he'd said too much when she didn't say anything. He felt tears wet his chest just as he heard her whisper, "I love you so much it scares me." Pulling back just enough he could look into her eyes, he kissed her tears away.

"Don't ever be afraid of love, Layla. It's the most precious gift of all. I love you too, but it doesn't scare me, it empowers me. That's what I want my love to do for you— I want it to be your refuge, your safe place in every storm, and the whisper in your spirit that promises your heart it's okay to be brave, that you should never be afraid to jump because you trust your Masters will be there to catch you if you fall."

Pulling her back against his chest, he smiled when she took a deep breath before going limp as she let herself slide into an exhausted sleep.

Cash lay there holding his sweet woman for hours, contemplating how lucky he was to have found her. He and his brothers had doubted there was a woman out there who they would all agree was perfect for them. And if she did exist, what were the odds of finding her? But his grandmother's wisdom had once again proven to be inspired. Cash could hardly wait for Layla to meet the older woman and knew they were going to be fast friends.

When his cock had finally slipped from her channel, he felt the warm rush of their combined releases flow from her body, and the Navajo warrior in his DNA wanted to beat his chest because that mark was a sign of victory. He meant what he said—he could hardly wait to start a family with Layla. He thought back over the times they'd made love to her and realized they used condoms infrequently. Even though that was completely out of character for them, he found himself having to tamp down the small seed of hope that blossomed in his soul. *Wouldn't it be a blessing to find out she already carried our child?*

Pushing that thought aside, he let his mind turn to his little sister. There was something haunting her—he could see it in her eyes, but he wasn't sure how to approach her yet. He didn't want to gloss over or ignore her pain, but he didn't want to pressure her either. There had to be a way to find a balance.

There was something very significant about the situation with Noah Drummond, something about him was tripping all Cash's alarms in a very big way. His intuition was rarely wrong, and it was shouting to him there was a reason Alex Lamont had taken up the younger man's cause. Alex didn't defend someone unless he knew they deserved his protection—simply owing a favor wouldn't be enough to elicit the response Cash had witnessed the other night. But what possible connection could there be between a former SEAL team-leader and a photographer? That, no doubt, was the million-dollar question.

LAYLA CAME AWAKE slowly when a chill went through her. She'd been sleeping so soundly, all toasty warm. When the warmth seemed to simply disappear, she was left looking around for penguins. Her eyes finally focused and the first things to emerge from the fog were the two men standing beside the bed. Cash and Clay were both looking at her, but it was Clay's impish grin that snagged her attention when Cash cleared his throat.

"Good morning, love. Just for the record, I was going to let you sleep a bit longer, but little brother wanted to play—he is the one who uncovered you. He's the reason your lovely skin is turning blue." Cash chuckled and leaned down to kiss her. "I have a few things to do today and need to leave for a bit, so I'm leaving you in Clay's loving care. Collin is holed up in his office finishing a project, so you shouldn't expect to see him before this evening. What did you have planned for today?"

Blinking to try to gain some sort of control over her scattered thoughts, Layla knew she must have failed to eliminate her confused look when both men smiled at her indulgently.

"Well, oh shit, it's Monday. What time is it? Crapping alley cats, I'm going to be late. I hate being late." She had started scrambling to get out of bed, but Clay placed his massive hand on her shoulder to keep her in place. She blinked at him in her confusion. "What?"

Clay sat on the edge of the bed as he answered her question, "Babe, it's very early. Please settle back and relax. I want to spend some time with you. I missed you last night." When she saw the sincerity in his eyes, she didn't hesitate to crawl up into his lap. He held her tightly and kissed the top of her head. "God, I love you, baby girl. You are just fucking incredible."

Layla saw Cash move into her peripheral view, then felt him kiss the top of her head.

"Clay, text me when you know what her plans are today." Then he redirected his attention to her. "Don't work too hard today, love. I know you have a meeting up at ShadowDance with Alex and Zach, so please take one of our vehicles. It snowed just a bit, and the roads won't be terribly slick, but the tires on your car are deplorable. We'll be discussing that little car this evening, love. We need to get you and Collin to come to some kind of mutual agreement about the situation."

She watched as he walked toward the door and could have sworn she heard him mutter something about peace in the Middle East being a more reasonable goal.

After she heard the door close, Clay gave her a quick squeeze before saying, "Come on, baby, time for more water sports." He carried her into the bath, and she noticed the room was already steamed up and warm from the shower he had obviously started before waking her. *Oh boy, I'm going to be spoiled rotten in no time.*

Clay shampooed and conditioned her hair—his long

fingers massaging her scalp was almost enough to make her come, it felt so wonderful. She gasped when he pressed her breasts against the wall of windows. Her nipples tightened into stiff peaks when she realized she was completely exposed to anyone walking through their backyard or up the driveway. The idea she could be seen made her pussy even wetter.

"The possibility you might be seen as I fuck you from behind turns you on, doesn't it, baby? I can feel how your body responded, you know, and that's a fucking turn-on for me as well. Here, let me help you lift your leg up. That's right, put your foot on this bench. Perfect. Now I'm going to show you exactly how much I missed you last night. I'm going to take you right here—right now. I need to feel you wrapping my cock in your sweet, pulsing pussy, baby."

Clay positioned the head of his cock at her opening and started a leisurely push and retreat that was going to drive her completely insane, it was so slow. Each move was a deliberate caress along her needy vaginal walls.

"Oh God, please, I need you to... oh please... more." Even to her ears, she sounded breathless and needy, but it must have been enough to flip some switch in Clay. He pushed in balls deep and shoved a hand between her lower abdomen and the glass. When his talented fingers started to circle her clit, she felt her climax building like a wave gathering energy from the sea before it crashes onto the shore. Clay began stroking her, his cock moving in deep, rapid thrusts, and she knew he was close.

"It's a magic carpet ride, baby... come fly with me." He punctuated his words by pressing her clit between his strong fingers, and she heard herself screaming as the wave that had been building pulled her under. Her orgasm was like rolling around in a tornado of water, and she wasn't sure which way was up or down. Layla could only ride it out and hope it brought her safely back to shore.

Chapter 15

W HEN LAYLA WALKED into Alex and Zach Lamont's beautiful sunlit office, the first thing she noticed was her smile was met by their stern expressions. Deciding to meet the challenge head-on, she didn't bother to sit in the proffered chair, just spoke up clearly.

"Good afternoon, bosses. Care to share what your scowls are about?"

Surprisingly, it was Zach who spoke first, "Why are you still driving that POS? I thought we had a deal? It snowed—*again*—last night you know. Do your men know you drove that rattletrap up the mountain today?"

Oh, snap, they're going to rat me out, just as sure as the sun's gonna set in the west tonight. Taking a deep breath and bringing herself up to her full height, she crossed her arms under her ample breasts. To their credit, their eyes stayed fixed on her face—smart men, her bosses.

"Well, thanks for your concern... I think. Yes, we did have a deal, but as I'm sure you are aware, car shopping takes time, and I've been busy working for two very demanding bosses." She smiled sweetly at them, and even though Alex's posture didn't change, she was sure she'd seen his lips twitch.

"And to answer your last question, no, the Red Cloud brothers do not know I drove my car up here this morning.

The vehicles they left for me were... well, let's just say I wasn't comfortable with any of the options. And for heaven's sake, there is only a light dusting of snow, and I'm not planning to be here that long, so it's not likely to be a problem unless someone rats me out." She glared right back at them both, and at least this time, they had the good sense to act at least a little contrite.

What she wasn't about to mention was she'd promised all three men she wouldn't drive her little car today, but damn... they'd left her a fucking Hummer, a Porsche, and something called a Lexus LF-CH. When she had gotten into the black Lexus, it had looked so intimidating, she'd hadn't even tried to find the ignition. What was with those guys, anyway? They couldn't leave her a simple vehicle, something she wouldn't have to be a computer engineer to operate? Damn it all to hell.

Their meeting had gone well after that, but she hadn't missed their sudden interest in their phones before she made her way out of their office. They'd been typing furiously, and she was sure the rat bastards were texting one of *her men*, no doubt.

Sighing deeply as she closed the door, she turned to see Kat smiling at her. Her new friend wrapped her hand around Layla's wrist and started dragging her toward the kitchen.

"Come on, I am dying to hear all about your Red Cloud weekend. And if I don't talk to some adult besides those two bossy husbands of mine, I'm going to be certifiable by nightfall."

Layla laughed and let herself be led into the Lamonts' massive kitchen, not giving another thought to the trouble that waited at the bottom of ShadowDance Mountain. The next two hours flew by as she and Kat traded bossy men stories and giggled about all the ways those men could send you sailing over the moon.

Kat was thrilled to hear Ilaina Red Cloud had moved home. It seemed both Katarina and her best friend, now her sister-in-law, Jenna had always liked the youngest Red Cloud. Kat was already trying to figure out ways she and Ilaina could work together that would benefit both of their businesses. Katarina Lamont built and maintained websites for a variety of high-profile clients, and from what Layla had seen, she was incredibly talented. Layla told Kat how impressed she'd been with everything she'd seen Kat had done and promised to mention it to Ilaina when she saw her that night at dinner.

Jenna waddled through the kitchen, and they all giggled at her self-description. Kat shook her head and chastised, "You're not a whale. There is only one baby in there, so stop whining to me, sister mine." Kat laughed at her friend, and after carrying triplets, Layla figured Kat was going to be a hard sell for sympathy. When Jenna winced when she sat down, Kat raised an eyebrow at her. "What was that? Are you having contractions?"

"No, they are just Braxton-Hicks, and thanks for saying that out freaking loud when we are smack in the middle of Spy-Central. You know whoever is in the Crow's Nest is probably already talking to my husband, right?" Jenna rolled her eyes and turned to Layla.

"I hope someone warned you about this damned place. My brothers are... well, let's just say they're a fracking boatload overcautious because they objected the last time I referred to them as 'fuck-stick paranoid bastards.'" She laughed and held her large baby belly, looking at Kat. "Boy, they got really ticked, and I really was just kidding... mostly. Yikes, Colt was about fifty-two sorts of pissed too.

Man, I got a paddling to remember for that one." Shaking her head at the memory, she returned her gaze to Layla.

"Anyway, this place is wired for sight and sound in ways that make the CIA and Homeland Security headquarters look like Romper Room. If you fart, somebody in the nest blabs."

Kat laughed and looked at her watch. "Yep, I'd say your honey is due about... now." All three women burst out in hysterical giggles as Colt stalked into the room. He looked at them, his confusion clearly written in his stern expression and asked "What?" That was all it took to send them into another round of laughter. He finally shook his head and pointed toward the windows.

"Layla, honey, it's gotten dark, you need to be headed home. I can't imagine your men are going to be happy about you driving that cracker-box on roller skates you call a car up here, and they're probably going to paddle your ass for staying so long, you had to drive down in the dark. I'd drive you myself, but I don't want Jenna to be alone when she's having contractions she conveniently failed to mention. Thank God the guys called."

Layla was already scrambling to put on her coat and grab her purse. She quickly said goodbye to her friends and headed out to her car. She really hadn't intended to stay so long, but damn it, she'd been enjoying her friend's company and wasn't accustomed to having to answer to anyone. *Yeah, that's going to take some getting used to.*

Driving down the mountain as quickly as she could safely, she noticed the steep road had indeed gotten incredibly slick. How had that happened? It hadn't even snowed again. Damn, she was going to be in so much trouble. Just as she was approaching the scariest of the sharp switchbacks, she noticed bright lights approaching her from the rear.

The vehicle was obviously much larger than her small car and didn't appear to be slowing down. When she tried to pull to the side so the larger vehicle could pass, the driver simply positioned himself directly behind her and narrowed the distance between them until she was completely blinded by the brilliant white headlights.

By the time she realized how close she was to the curve and stomped down on her well-worn brakes, her smooth tires were useless. She didn't even think her tiny car had slowed any before she heard the haunting sound of metal grinding against metal. Just as she felt her car pushing its way through the railing, she felt herself jerked by her shoulder belt but not before her forehead hit the steering wheel with enough force to make her see stars. *That's what I get for buying a car too old to have properly functioning airbags.*

Layla felt her car listing precariously over the edge and prayed it would stay balanced. She waited for the driver who had blinded her to approach her vehicle, but the large truck just paused for a few seconds, then took off down the mountain. *No! Don't leave me like this!*

She tried to search for her phone, but every small movement made her car teeter on the edge and sent her into a panic. Vowing she needed to stay conscious, she tried reciting every single thing she'd ever been forced to memorize, but her head hurt so badly, she finally rationalized it would be alright to close her eyes just for a few seconds, and she let the darkness pull her under.

CASH COULDN'T REMEMBER the last time he'd been as pissed

off as he'd been when he returned home and discovered Layla had driven her own car up to her meeting with the Lamonts. Damn it, he'd been home two fucking hours. *Where the fuck is she?* He'd called her phone dozens of times without getting an answer and only gotten angrier. Collin walked into the room and looked around.

"Where's Layla?" Cash had just been explaining the situation when Clay walked in.

"What did Layla drive today? Nothing seems to have been moved. I left her keys for everything in the garage downstairs because I didn't want her slipping on the stone walkway down to the shed." Clay's puzzled look told him his youngest brother had given her a choice, and it seemed that's where the problem had started.

By the time he'd updated Clay, they were all three seething. Cash was just pulling on his jacket when his phone rang, and the hair on the back of his neck stood straight up. A feeling of cold terror raced up his spine, and it took every ounce of courage he had to answer his phone to what he feared was going to be a life-altering conversation. Seeing Dylan Marshall's name on the caller I.D. screen sent Cash's heart to the bottom of his stomach. "Cash Red Cloud" was all he managed to get out.

"Cash, Dylan. Layla's been in an accident. We're just loading her up, and the EMS will be heading to the hospital with her in five. She's got a bad bump on her head, and she's floating in and out of consciousness, but she is asking for you and your brothers. Drive safe, I don't want to work another accident tonight, got it?" Dylan was a good friend, and Cash appreciated his no-nonsense manner and his concern. They'd all grown up together, and Dylan wouldn't have any trouble remembering all the crazy-assed driving they'd all done as teens.

"On our way. Thanks for taking care of her." Cash pocketed his phone and shouted to his brothers to get their coats, he'd update them on the way. Swinging by to grab Ilaina on their way to the garage, the three men told their sister what little they knew.

Fifteen minutes later, they walked through the doors of the emergency room of Climax's small hospital. It wasn't a large facility, but the equipment was state-of-the-art, thanks to hefty donations and backing from the Lamonts. Cash made a quick mental note talk to Collin about adding the rural health care facility to the list of worthy causes supported by the charitable foundation his brother had founded a couple of years earlier.

Before he made his way to the desk, he was met by a young woman who introduced herself as Dr. Bree Creed-Jantz. He remembered Jamie and Ethan had missed the Grand Opening because they had only returned that afternoon from their honeymoon. Cash hadn't met their wife yet, but he had heard a lot of positive things about her from Alex and Zach.

Reaching out to shake the hand she offered, he noticed she didn't hesitate to include his brothers in their conversation, so she had obviously already been told they'd be arriving. Cash knew he spoke for all of them when he said, "It's nice to meet you, we've heard a lot about you from the Lamonts. Congratulations, by the way. Now, how's our girl?"

Bree smiled at them before speaking, "Aha, another Dom..." then glancing at his brothers, she added, "or three... Well, as it happens, I know just how to communicate with you." Turning she started down a short hall.

"Follow me, I'll update you on the way. Layla has a serious concussion, but right now, the only thing on her mind is the three of you. We haven't really been able to get her to work with us, so we haven't been able to adequately assess her condition. I'm hoping she'll be able to focus once she knows you have arrived." The pretty young doctor stopped in front of a closed door and turned to face them.

"I want you to be prepared because it's important you not upset her any more than she is already. She has a horrible bruise on her forehead I'm sure is going to result in two shiners before all is said and done. We've cast her right wrist because the X-ray shows a small fracture, and she wasn't settled enough that I felt comfortable with a simple splint. At this point, I'd say her memory is maxing at about three minutes, and while that is up from the thirty seconds reported by the first man on the scene, I'm sure you'll agree it's a long way from where we want to be."

"Can you tell me who the first man on the scene was? I'd like to speak with him personally, we owe him a huge debt." Cash was curious who had found Layla and really did intend to thank the man personally.

Bree flipped open a small spiral notebook, then looked shyly up at Collin. "Sorry, I've heard you are a computer guy, so I'm sure I seem pretty backward to you." She shrugged before adding, "I grew up in very remote locations, and well, old habits die hard, and it seems hand-held technology is not in our budget this year."

Cash had to smile at how quickly the knowledgeable professional façade had fallen away, replaced by a beautiful young woman—with nothing more than a simple shoulder shrug.

Collin stepped up and took her hand in his. "How about we strike a bargain, you take care of our sweet girl, and I'll see what I can do about helping you out with your tech challenges, deal?" She smiled and nodded before returning her attention to the small notepad.

"Let's see, I talked to him earlier. Oh yes, here it is," she said, flipping through the small pages of her notebook. "A local, Noah Drummond. From what I heard, if he hadn't quickly secured her vehicle, it would have gone off the ledge and dropped over a hundred feet. Thank God he had ropes and climbing equipment with him. You'll have to ask Dylan, but it's my understanding he called someone at The Club via radio because he'd lost his cell phone when he was securing the rope to the undercarriage of her car. He managed to keep her calm until help arrived... wish he'd have ridden down here with her." Cash almost chuckled when she'd muttered the last words under her breath.

By the time the doctor stopped speaking, there were more questions than answers floating through Cash's mind—and one of the most significant was why would a photographer have a radio capable of patching him through to someone at The ShadowDance Club? He also wondered how he was going to explain to his sister they all now owed a huge debt of gratitude to the one man who sent her reeling at the mere mention of his name. Oblivious to his inner struggle, Bree opened the door to Layla's room, and Cash was stunned at his first look at their woman. Layla was battered and bruised... and spitting mad. Their little tigress was looking at a male nurse with mutiny in her eyes.

"I'm telling you, my boyfriends are gonna be pissed if y'all don't stop that nonsense."

"Miss, please... I'm only trying to help you change into something that isn't covered in mud. It's not personal, I assure you."

Cash actually felt sorry for the young man who was

obviously being steamrolled by his injured patient.

"Did I tell you I have boyfriends? They are going to be mad at you... if I can remember to tell them... what's your name again?" If he hadn't been so damned worried about her, it might have been funny, but as it was, he was fighting back an emotional wave he feared was going to swamp him at any moment. *Oh yeah, you're a big bad SEAL, and your fixin' to cry like a fucking baby the first time your woman gets hurt.*

Finally getting himself together, he stepped into the room. "Love, you've taken another decade *or two* off our lives." When she looked up and saw the three of them, it was as if someone deflated her. Several seconds later, she appeared to let go of the emotions he assumed she'd been holding back and broke out in soul deep sobs.

He knew she'd stayed strong until she didn't have to any longer, and his heart swelled with love because she'd known they'd take care of her. There was no better feeling for a Dom than to know his sub trusted him completely. He and Collin made their way to her bedside while Clay took the clean shirt from the nurse and assured him they'd get her changed into it right away.

"Come on, baby, let us change you out of that wet shirt." Clay approached her before the door was even closed behind the nurse.

"Okay. I'm cold. Did you bring that with you? That was so sweet of you." Cash looked up at Bree who shrugged as if that confirmed what she'd told them earlier.

"No, love, the nice nurse who just left brought it in for you. Come on now, off with that wet shirt." Cash knew there was no reason to scold her about driving her car while she was in this condition—upsetting her further would be counterproductive, and she'd never remember it, anyway. When he glanced up at Collin, Cash was shocked to see his brother was white as a sheet. Cash often forgot both he and Clay were accustomed to seeing injuries, but Collin's line of work offered him little exposure to the world outside those of his own creation.

Dr. Bree followed his line of sight and bless her heart, she didn't miss a beat. Linking her arm through Collin's, she asked, "Could I trouble you to come down the hall with me for a few minutes? I need help with the paperwork for Layla. I'd also love to give you my contact information for when you're ready for that technology chat."

Cash had to give the woman credit—she did indeed know exactly how to handle a Dom.

Chapter 16

I LAINA FOUND HERSELF herded into a waiting room that was rapidly filling with people, some she recognized, but many of the faces were completely unfamiliar. Suddenly realizing how long she'd been gone from her hometown, she made her way over to a corner and tried to stay out of the way and disappear. After learning the hard way how badly being open and friendly in public could turn out, she'd quickly learned to avoid any public exposure that wasn't tightly controlled by her agency. If her brothers ever got wind of what the past year had been like, there would be no living with any of them. As if she'd thought trouble into existence, she raised her eyes and locked gazes with none other than Noah Drummond.

For a few beats of her heart, she worried her knees were going to fold out from under her, but she stiffened her spine and quickly looked away. Hopefully, he'd take the hint and leave. She doubted she'd be that lucky, but a girl could always hope, right? Ilaina hadn't realized she was staring at the floor until a pair of scuffed, but very expensive loafers came into her view.

"Ilaina, it's good to see you. I wish it were under better circumstances."

She knew she must have looked surprised when she jerked her gaze up to meet his. She was amazed he already knew about Layla's accident. *Wow, the grapevine is obviously on fire tonight.*

"How… um, how did you know?" She cursed herself for the vibrato in her voice. It always happened when she was extremely nervous, and with her luck, the small tell would be something he'd remember.

"I was the first person on the scene, *Cara.* I was on my way up to see the Lamonts when I came upon her car. She's very lucky, she nearly went off the ledge, and at that point on the road, it's at least a hundred feet straight down."

He reached up and stroked his fingers down the side of her face in a move so comforting, yet so overly familiar, it startled her. When her brain finally caught up and pulled the reins from her heart, she quickly stepped back and away from his touch.

She felt her heart squeeze when she realized he'd called her by the nickname he'd given her so many years ago. Noah had been the only one who had called her anything but Lainy. One night as they'd watched the fireflies dancing in the trees in her backyard, he finally explained why he called her by the sweet name since they'd been little more than junior high school students. He explained he'd chosen the name after he'd learned it meant "face" in Spanish since it sounded so pretty and reminded him of her pretty face.

"Why were you in town? I mean, how long? Well, shit. I should just say thank you and let it go, so… "Thank you. I assume you are the one who called the authorities, so our family appreciates your help." She hadn't noticed Cash standing alongside her until he spoke.

"He did a lot more than call the authorities, Lainy. He secured her car and kept Layla calm until she could be removed from the vehicle. His quick actions likely saved our woman's life. My brothers and I are deeply indebted to you, Noah. Thank you just doesn't seem like enough..." Cash's words trailed off, and Ilaina could see how close her brother was to an emotional edge.

Looking back at Noah, she noted he wasn't looking at Cash, he was focused on her. She was startled by the sound of a woman's airy voice and even more taken aback to realize it belonged to her.

"Is this true?"

"Yes. *Cara*, I'd like to speak with you before you leave, but first I need to have a word with your brother." Noah nodded his head to the side, and she watched as Cash followed him a few steps away.

Watching as they spoke quietly, she saw Cash's body stiffen and stepped forward, placing her hand on his muscular back.

"Are you okay?" She and Cash had always been close. He'd been her knight in shining armor her entire life. Her parents had laughed and said they could have turned her over to her seven-year-old brother when they'd brought her home from the hospital, and he'd have happily raised her all by himself.

Cash nodded and then turned back to Noah.

"Please make sure you give that information to Dylan. I'm not sure what it means, but my gut tells me it's important."

Noah nodded, then said, "I agree, and it's never a good idea to ignore a gut feeling. I'm sure those have saved your life as often as they've saved mine." For just a second Ilaina was as puzzled by the remark as Cash appeared to be, but then they were interrupted by a nurse calling Cash back to Layla's room.

"Thanks again for all you did for Layla. Please leave

your cell number with Lainy so we can call you if we have any more questions about your conversation with her." With those words, Cash rushed off down the hall.

When she looked at Noah in question, he just shrugged.

"I'd be happy to talk to you about it, but I see Dylan is here. I want to catch him before he gets swamped. Can I see your phone please?" When she numbly handed it over, he quickly dialed a number, and she heard the phone in his pocket beep.

"Now you have my number, *Cara*. Please share it with your brothers and please feel free to use it any time you would like to talk." He seemed to study her for a few seconds before continuing, "I have some things I need to explain to you, but I know this is not the time. Go check on your sweet friend and be there for your brothers—I'm sure they have missed you even more than I have."

Ilaina hadn't been aware of him holding her wrist in his warm grip after he'd handed her phone back. The tips of his calloused finger were drawing soothing circles over her pulse-point, and when he released her to move toward Sheriff Marshall, she felt as if the warmth in the room had been suddenly sucked away.

Oh, Ilaina, you are so screwed.

WHEN CASH HAD been called back to Layla's room, he'd been terrified she'd taken a turn for the worse. He'd seen a lot of soldiers with concussions and knew the injuries were notorious for being unpredictable and even deadly on occasion. He hated leaving Lainy with Noah, but it couldn't be helped. Hopefully, Drummond would be busy making his report to Dylan Marshall, and Lainy would find her way to Layla's room.

Rounding the corner into her room, Cash noticed Collin standing at the side of the bed with his arms crossed over his chest, looking like he'd swallowed a lemon and Clay sitting on the other side, trying to calm the distraught woman battling to get out of the bed.

"But I have to find Cash, he is probably looking for me, and I don't want him to worry. I heard there was a bad wreck on the mountain, and I don't want him to think it was me. *Please.* I promise I'll just be gone a minute."

Cash could only imagine how hard she'd be to round up in the hospital if she ever made it out of their sight.

Collin looked up at him, shaking his head, and Cash had to fight the urge to laugh. Clearly, the strictest Dom of them was waging an internal battle to stand by and not just order Layla to cooperate. No doubt Dr. Bree had explained how ineffective that tactic would be, and judging by the look on Collin's face, the news hadn't set well.

Just then Layla looked up and saw him and squealed so loud, Cash was sure there would be a stampede to the door, and he was right. She started clamoring to get out of the bed, so he stepped up and sat down next to her and pulled her onto his lap. His heart melted when she immediately settled down and snuggled against him.

"Oh, I'm so glad you finally got here. I've been so worried about you. Did you know there was a bad wreck up on the mountain? I was worried it was you. Why were you up wandering around? You should be lying down taking it easy. Did you get run off the road by that big truck?"

She was asking questions and changing things around at such an alarming rate, Cash was having trouble keeping up. He heard Collin explaining to Bree that Layla had gone from fearing Cash would think the wreck was her to thinking it had been him in consecutive sentences. But this mention of a truck was the first she'd mentioned that part of the story since she'd told Noah Drummond about being forced off the road by the blinding lights of a large truck.

"I think it was the same truck that tried to scare me the other night, but I really don't know. My head hurts so much, but every time I go to sleep, someone wakes me up. Can I sleep here? You won't let them push me off the road again, will you? Boy, I'm really thirsty, too. Did I eat lunch? Boy, I'm tired." And just like that, she was fast asleep.

Bree giggled and said, "Even though we always worry about patients with severe concussions, they can sure be a hoot once we know they don't have any brain bleeds. Her scans all came back clear, but I'd like to keep her overnight to be sure. Cash, if you could stay with her, that would be helpful. She seems to settle the most when you are in the room. I'm just guessing, but I'd wager you were the first one of the three of you to meet her, right?"

When he nodded, she smiled, then started herding out the other staff who had rushed in at Layla's high-pitched squeal. Cash looked up as Dylan Marshall, who was leaning against the wall, moved closer as the room emptied out.

"Did you hear her?"

"I did, and that jives with what she told Noah at the scene. I want to check with Bree, but from what I've heard, sometimes the confusion isn't immediate after a head injury, and if that's right, her report to Drummond would be even more credible."

Collin and Clay were clearly confused by their conversation, so he and Dylan brought them up to speed quickly and as quietly as possible, hoping Layla would get a bit of rest before they had to wake her again.

"Noah said he met several vehicles on his way up the mountain, but he hadn't really paid much attention because he'd been concentrating on driving on the slick road. But he said Layla was adamant a large truck had caused her to wreck. She just didn't understand why the truck stopped, and she felt like the driver was looking at her before it had simply sped down the mountain. Had she mentioned anything to you about a previous incident before just now? Because that was new information for me." Dylan pulled a small iPad from inside his coat and tapped so hard on the screen, Cash almost cringed.

Collin stepped forward and shook his head before reaching for the device. "Damnit, Dylan, you're going to put your Jolly Green Giant fingers right through the fucking screen. What are you trying to do? Beat the poor thing into submission?"

"What? Well, the damned thing doesn't work very well for me for some reason. It likes Mia better—it's fucking Benedict Arnold in a box. Anyway, I was sending a message to my deputies to keep their ears to the ground and be on the lookout for a large dark-colored truck that doesn't belong to a local."

Collin had the iPad in hand and quickly finished typing the message Dylan had started. When he was through, he turned to Dylan.

"It likes Mia better because that sweet wife of yours doesn't beat on it like it's some kind of African drum issuing a call to arms. Come by the house someday, and I'll give you the iPad for Dummies crash course. It'll save you a lot of grief and probably a lot of money as well."

Dylan laughed and agreed to meet up with them to-morrow at their home. They assured him they'd be taking

Layla home with them so they could take care of her. Just as Dylan opened the door to leave, Kat Lamont swept through the open door.

"Oh my God, is she okay? I couldn't believe it when I heard she'd had an accident on the way back to you. How long does she have to stay here? Do you need me to bring her anything? Is Bree her doctor? I know she was planning to drive really slow, so I can't imagine how she had trouble. Did one of you find her? What time was it? God, I hope she didn't have to lie in the cold very long." She shivered and started to open her mouth to speak again but was interrupted when her husbands both stepped around the tiny blonde.

"Katarina, I don't know how you do it, love, but I do believe you just set a new personal record—six questions and three topic changes without taking a breath. Impressive, but perhaps a bit overwhelming, don't you think?" Alex pulled her into his arms and kissed the top of her head before looking down at her indulgently. Looking up at each of them, he asked, "How is she?"

Collin stepped forward and explained what Bree had told them. Both Alex and Zach nodded, listening intently, but Kat had moved to sit next to him and was slowly stroking Layla's hair back from her face in the soothing strokes of a mother. When Cash smiled at her, he saw she had big tears in her eyes.

"She is so sweet and fun... and she's completely smitten with the three of you, you know?" She paused for a moment, then sighed. "I was so hoping I'd finally made a friend some asshat wasn't trying to hurt."

"Katarina, language. I swear, we can't take her anywhere." Alex's words were tempered by his smile, and when Cash looked over at Zach, he saw the big man wink

AVERY GALE

at his tiny sweetheart of a wife. Everyone laughed quietly when Kat cringed, then shrugged.

"Sorry, but I'm a passionate person." Glancing at her husbands, she added, "And it's all because of you, my loving husbands."

Alex shook his head. "Good save, love. Now, perhaps you'd like to ask your questions one at a time?"

Cash let his brothers give everyone the updated information while he kept quiet, hoping Layla wouldn't be disturbed as he held her against his chest. She hadn't stirred, and it was very satisfying to feel her curled against him like a contented kitten.

After everyone had been shooed out by the nursing staff and Layla roused so she could identify the current President of the United States and the date, he settled her once more and lay alongside her on the bed. Collin and Clay left to take Lainy back home and look at Layla's car. He'd also heard Collin speaking with Zach about enlisting Mitch Grayson's help to expand Layla's background check to see if they could identify who was targeting the Red Clouds' woman. Cash was too busy assessing everything that had happened to sleep, so he just held her in his arms and thanked the Great Spirit for the opportunity.

He was still frustrated she hadn't driven something safer, but in all honesty, if she had, she might not have fared as well. If she'd been in a vehicle she wasn't accustomed to, she might well have lost control sooner and not had the guardrail to slow her down. He shuddered at the thought of how differently this day could have ended.

Chapter 17

L AYLA HAD BEEN ready to climb the walls for days. All three of the Red Cloud brothers had hovered until she'd nearly taken off each of their heads. She wasn't sure she'd have been allowed to return to work yet if it hadn't been for Lainy and Cora Red Cloud's help.

Cora and her husbands had arrived the day she'd been dismissed from the hospital and stayed for several days, helping keep her entertained and corralled. She'd been grateful for their company and for keeping the men distracted, so they hadn't smothered her with their attention. Cora was a pistol, and it was easy to see where Ilaina had gotten her fierce independence as well as her incredible beauty.

She'd enjoyed the time she spent with the elder Red Clouds and had nearly cried when she'd watched the family interact during their meals together. Losing contact with her large extended family had been almost more than Layla had been able to bear, but she'd thrown herself into proving to them she could not only survive but thrive as well. It had been her determination to prove herself that had gotten her through.

Tori and Trace had been out of town when she'd had her accident, but since their return, her sweet friend had stopped by the Red Clouds' each day to check on her.

Layla was fairly certain her friend was pregnant, but she hadn't had a chance to ask her. There hadn't been more than a few seconds when they hadn't been surrounded by other people. Layla might be outspoken, but she certainly wasn't rude, and she understood the value of discretion. She knew the Bartells were trying to conceive, and she could hardly wait until the couple had good news to share. Layla planned to be the best *aunt* there ever was. Since Tori and Trace were both only children, and Layla was basically an orphan, she'd nominated herself as "aunt" to their future children.

Looking around the motel, she was amazed at what had been completed in the past few days. The facility was nearly ready for guests, and Layla could barely contain her enthusiasm. They'd started taking reservations a couple of days ago, and her assistant manager had stepped up in fine fashion while Layla had been recovering.

She noticed a piece of string hanging from the light fixture in her office and wondered how it could have gotten there. Glancing around she saw a small wooden stepladder and decided to investigate. Her wrist was still in a cast, but the ladder appeared to be stable, and she was too curious to wait for someone else to happen along.

Just as she reached for the string she heard a loud snap that sounded like wood splintering, then the ladder went out from under her. She heard herself scream, then it felt like her right ankle had been locked in a vise before someone hit it with a hammer. *Holy fucking shit that hurts! And how am I going to get to the phone I left on my desk?*

CLAY HAD BEEN working on the last of the security cameras when he heard a woman's scream. He knew Layla was the only woman in the building, so the sound had sent him into a panic. When he ran into her office, he found her on the floor, clutching her ankle and crying softly. He barely glanced at the small wooden ladder but noticed both back legs looked as if they had been cut part way through, then broke the rest of the way off. After checking to be sure Layla wasn't injured anywhere else, he sent a quick message to his brothers and made a quick call to the hospital's emergency department to let them know he was on his way in with her.

"I don't understand it, that ladder is brand new. How could it have broken so easily?" Layla's question was already weighing heavily on his mind. He wasn't moving the ladder until his brothers and Dylan had a chance to look at it.

Scooping her up into his arms, Clay made his way to the door but returned to lean down so she could retrieve her phone and purse before heading out to his truck. Collin came skidding into the parking lot just as they approached his truck.

"Oh, sweetheart, what's happened to you?"

Clay could count on one hand the number of times he'd heard that tone from his older brother, and you could be sure it had never been spoken to him. He had to suppress his laugh because it really was a kick to hear Collin speaking sweetly to a woman other than their mother or sister.

Collin had always been such a strict Dom, he rarely came across as compassionate, and that had worried Clay and Cash when they'd first discussed sharing a woman. They'd wanted a loving relationship like their parents, but they hadn't been convinced Collin would be onboard.

Cash met them at the hospital, and they all waited while Layla's broken ankle was set and cast. Clay had felt so sorry for her. He remembered the many times he'd broken bones and knew she was replaying her day, wishing she could rewind and start over. Six weeks sounded like forever when a part of your body was being wrapped in plaster and fiberglass.

Now that she had a wrist and an ankle in casts, there was no way she could safely return to her small guesthouse at ShadowDance. As far as he was concerned, aside from the fact she hadn't been hurt any worse, they now had the perfect excuse to keep her in their home.

Layla had been given mild painkillers and was happily chatting up everyone within earshot as they'd stood outside the small cubicle where she was currently waiting for the cast to cure. Her chatter had been amusing, but once she'd started giggling with Bree about having three "hot honeys," they had to intervene.

Collin had gone instantly pale, and Clay and Cash had laughed out loud at his mortification. For a genius, kinky multi-millionaire Dom involved in a polyamorous relationship, he could really be an uptight prude sometimes—and damn if that didn't amuse the shit out of Clay.

By the time they returned home, Layla was out cold, and they'd all been relieved because she'd been little miss Chatty Cathy for over an hour. Suddenly, Clay had a new appreciation for Alex and Zach's exasperation with Kat's ability to rapid-fire questions seemingly without ever stopping to take a breath. Hell, it had been exhausting trying to keep up with the subject changes alone. They elevated her leg and tucked her in on the family room sofa, so they could keep track of her while they made dinner.

Not long after they'd moved to the kitchen, they heard a soft ringing and realized it was coming from Layla's purse. When it continued to ring several more times, Cash had asked Lainy to fish the noisy thing out so they could make sure it hadn't been anything urgent.

There were dozens of missed calls, several were from Tori and Kat. Ilaina quickly noted their numbers and moved to the side to call the women so they wouldn't continue to worry. But there were several from a caller only showing up as unknown and a voicemail from that number as well. Collin dialed Layla's voice mail.

"I'm glad she had her passcode already stored in the memory. Now let's see who thinks it's so important, they've tried to call her twenty-two times in the past two hours, shall we?"

Cash stepped forward frowning. "I don't like snooping through her phone, but the sheer number of calls is disconcerting—let's see what's up." They had quickly moved into Collin's office and closed the door, so they didn't wake Layla.

The voice that came over the voicemail recording sent chills up Clay's spine, and the man's words were terrifying.

"So, precious niece of mine, how did you like the little bump and grind on the mountain road? Had you been meeting with those pervert bosses of yours? Were you headed back down to fuck the three guys you've been shacked up with? And how did you enjoy the slight adjustment I made to your ladder? That broken ankle ought to make running from me a bit tricky, don't you think?"

The next message began, and the man sounded even more menacing.

"Do you think you can just fucking not answer your phone and ignore me forever? You can run, but you can't hide. Bet you weren't expecting your favorite uncle to be out of prison quite so soon, were you? Let the games begin. You'll pay for what you did, don't think I've gone soft on your ass, you fucking traitor."

Clay thought Cash's words summed up his feeling up perfectly.

"Fuck! I'm going to kill the son of a bitch."

COLLIN SAVED THE messages and forwarded them to all three of their e-mail accounts as well as sending copies to Mitch Grayson and Dylan Marshall. He moved to his computer and was typing furiously, skimming everything he'd found online about Layla, looking for the word *uncle*. Nothing was tagging, and he couldn't figure it out. When his phone rang, he wasn't surprised to see Mitch's name on the I.D. and pushed the button for speakerphone.

"Talk to me."

Mitch's no-nonsense communication style was a throwback to his time in the military and his current job working with the Lamonts. Since Cash had worked for Alex and Zach a couple of times on contract jobs, Collin was aware of the Lamonts very lucrative side business— black ops for various governments, including their own.

"It has to be a juvie record, that's the only thing I can figure. I've got feelers out looking for those, but I think I may have stumbled onto something already. A man named Nick Lang was tried and convicted of murder in Houston several years ago. Seems the only witness was his minor niece. She testified, and he was convicted but was released recently on appeal—some fucking technicality that was completely aside from the fact the bastard beat a man to death in an alley.

"Hell, he can admit it now and never be retried because it would be double jeopardy to charge him again. If this is the guy, he is a loose cannon. His rap sheet is thirteen pages long. He's had a long string of arrests from the time he was ten years old and has a lot of nasty associates as well. I'll keep looking and get the full report, but I'm fairly certain this is our guy. Alex and Zach are sending you a couple of guys for perimeter patrol, and we'll update your security systems ASAP. Later." The call disconnected with a simple click before Collin had a chance to respond. *And everybody thinks programmers have poor communication skills.*

Collin went back to work on the computer, barely glancing over his shoulder at Cash.

"You guys protect Layla and Lainy, I'll keep digging. Make sure Dylan has patrols around here as often as possible. I'd love to see Lainy go visit Mom and the dads, but I doubt she'll agree to it." He suddenly stopped typing and looked at Cash and Clay. "We have to take care of this. We can't lose her. She's everything." When his brothers both nodded, he returned his attention to his keyboard.

Once he started searching various news sources for Nick Lang, the stories flooding his screen turned his stomach. The man was a cold-blooded killer who had openly bragged to associates about using his beautiful young niece as a distraction while he "worked."

Lang had been screaming threats at the young girl and her mother as deputies dragged him from the courtroom after his conviction. Then by all accounts, Layla's entire family had turned on her because she'd dared to cross one of their own. He read brief bits of her testimony, and when the prosecutor asked her why she'd agreed to testify, she simply answered, "It was the right thing to do."

Running his hands through his hair in frustration, he tried to imagine what kind of courage it took to make such a life-altering decision as a teenager. Then to be turned out onto the street by your entire family was almost unimaginable.

His heart nearly broke when he remembered her soft words as she'd sat on his lap one evening while his entire family had been laughing and watching an old comedy movie together. She'd leaned against his chest and whispered more to herself than anyone, "I've missed this so..."

He hadn't really understood her remark then, and now, he was kicking himself for not asking her to explain it. How the hell had she survived, let alone managed to finish high school and college? His respect and love for her just kept growing exponentially.

Chapter 18

L AYLA WAS TRYING to shift positions when a spear of pain shot through her leg, causing her to sit straight up, gasping for breath. It took a few seconds for her to realize she'd cried out and another few seconds to regain her bearings and realize she had tears streaming down her face. Blinking, she saw Cash run into the room with Clay and Ilaina close on his heels.

"Love, are you alright? I heard you yell." As he got closer, he must have seen the pain in her expression because he turned and asked his worried sister to retrieve the pain meds and a glass of water.

"Oh, wait, Ilaina, you don't need to be fetching things for me. I'll get them in a minute… I just need to catch my breath." She blinked again and looked down at her ankle. *What the hell?*

"Hold up. Why is my leg in that cast? Oh shit. How am I going to get down the stairs to the guesthouse? They get slick when it rains, and it's supposed to snow. I have to work, or I'm going to lose my job, and I really like my job. I have good bosses and like living in Climax, and I'm making friends and everything. And… whoa… why is the room spinning around… oh damn, I think I need to lie down for a minute before I get that medicine, and well, my stomach is not feeling so good."

She heard Clay say, "Get the crackers and Sprite—fast. And a cool rag for her forehead." She felt Cash's strong fingers holding her hand, and when Clay put the cool cloth on her forehead, she finally started to feel more settled.

"Just lie still, baby. You've had a lot of meds and nothing to eat, that's a not a good combination. We'll get some crackers in you and a couple of your pain pills, then some toast. I've been around this particular block a time or two, babe, so you gotta listen to me on this."

His fingers felt so good combing through her hair, and Cash's warm fingers were drawing small circles over the inside of her uncast wrist. God, she was a battered mess, and it was all her own fault.

By the time she'd followed all of Clay's advice, she was starting to feel almost normal even if she was feeling like she was a human balloon floating just a smidge above the bed where they'd settled her.

Layla was sure being carried to use the toilet and having Cash wait nearby for her was going to rank right up there with the most embarrassing moments of her life. He assured her she had no reason to be shy, but she'd still hidden her face in her hands the entire time.

Lying in bed, she looked at both men and could sense their unease. They were probably getting damned tired of her being such a clumsy pain in the ass. *Suck it up, Layla, you knew this would happen. Get dressed and call Tori. Hopefully, she'll let you stay with them until you can get another car and move on.*

She sat back up and started scooting to the edge and winced when her ankle started throbbing again. "Um... if you'll hand me my phone, I'll just give Tori a call and get out of your hair." *I can see you all have things on your mind, and I've been an awful lot of bother lately.* She was looking everywhere but at them because if she saw pity in their eyes, she was going to completely lose it, and damn, she hated crying.

When neither one of them moved, she finally looked up and saw nothing but confusion and compassion. Finally, Cash reached for her, and she couldn't do anything to stop the first tear from falling.

"Tell me what went through your head, my love because, for the life of me, I have no idea what's made you think you are a bother." When she jerked her gaze to his, he smiled and nodded. "Yes, you said it all out loud, but neither of us has a clue why." He paused for a few seconds, and she watched as he seemed to shift from lover to former SEAL before her eyes. "Your phone has been confiscated. We'll be getting you a new phone and a new number. Now, tell us all about Uncle Nick."

Layla felt as if the whole world shifted... and started spinning. Both men were suddenly surrounding her, their touch soothing as they laid her down flat—probably a good idea because she'd nearly taken a header off the bed. Finally focusing enough to speak, she answered.

"He's my mother's younger brother, but he was always the person who was kind of *in charge* because he's really not a nice person. But he's in prison, so I don't really know... wait. How did you know about him? Those records shouldn't include my name because I was so young." Suddenly, she felt like she was shaking from the inside out. If they were asking about her uncle, then something was seriously wrong.

Cash lifted her chin, forcing her to look at him before speaking.

"Love, for whatever reason, he is no longer in prison, and it looks as though he is behind the accidents you've been having. Your phone kept ringing last night—literally dozens of missed calls—so we checked it. Ilaina has called your friends, so they are no longer frantic with worry—word spreads fast in a small town, love."

He'd obviously seen her confusion. How would her friends have known she'd fallen and broken her ankle? She'd never lived in a small town and kept forgetting about the sense of family having close friends inspired.

"Now, all that being said, we also noted a lot of calls from an unknown number, so we checked the voice mail message from the same number." He held up his hand when she started to speak. "We weren't trying to snoop. We were concerned someone might have been trying to contact you with emergency information. What we heard was a couple of very threatening calls from a man who obviously means you harm. To keep you safe, we need as much information as you can give us about the situation. When you feel up to it, we'll take you downstairs, and you can speak with my team from ShadowDance via teleconference. The sooner this is resolved, the safer you and everyone else will be."

It just can't be. Why would they let him out? I saw him do it... I gave up everything to testify... and they fucking let him out? Why?

Those were the last thoughts she had before her mind simply shut down. It was easier to just not think anymore, and broken ankle or not, it was obviously time to leave. The minute her foot hit the ground, white-hot fire shot through her entire body, and she finally just let the darkness take her.

CLAY HAD WATCHED the entire scene unfold and wasn't that surprised when Layla made an ill-advised attempt to stand because she'd clearly checked out mentally—hell, the emotional overload would be too much for anyone. No doubt she had either forgotten about her broken ankle or simply not cared. He knew from experience the pain she'd felt when her foot had hit the ground had been devastating. He'd seen her eyes roll back seconds before she blacked out.

They'd caught her before she'd hit the floor, but it wasn't the physical pain that concerned him. It was the blank look he'd seen in her eyes just before she'd tried to stand. She'd obviously not been thinking clearly, and he'd bet his last nickel, she would run the first chance she had.

"One of us has to stay with her every minute—not only to protect her from her chicken shit uncle but to keep her from running. The minute you reassured her everyone else was safe, she checked out. Our woman will be terrified she's brought trouble here. She's going to try to leave to protect all of us."

Cash nodded in agreement. "Let's carry her back downstairs. We'll call her friends in, too. Hopefully, she'll listen to Tori. Make sure Trace is aware of the situation as well, I'm sure he'll want to accompany her. Same with Kat, we'll call Alex and Zach first."

Clay laughed. "I know just the thing. It's supposed to snow tonight, so let's ask Lainy to arrange a get-together for the girls. While they are enjoying the beach room, we can have a strategy session."

Cash agreed, and the minute Clay explained things to Lainy, she was onboard as well. In less than an hour, they had everything arranged and would be hosting a beach party the next afternoon. In the meantime, they'd make sure Layla wasn't left alone. Not that she had much hope of escaping when they'd conveniently "lost" her crutches, and all the keys to vehicles had vanished as well.

Chapter 19

LAYLA SAT AT the bar in the kitchen, chopping up veggies and mixing up dips for the beach party. She'd woken up this morning feeling a thousand times better, and once they figured out a way for her to wrap two casts, so she could take a quick shower, things had seemed even better.

Now she was sporting a pair of long, running shorts and a cropped t-shirt, so she felt ready for the beach party. She'd opted for a flip-flop since she still hadn't found where the men had hidden her crutches. Sometimes, wisdom was about choosing your battles and all things considered, being carried around by gorgeous hunks wasn't exactly a hardship.

Layla watched as Lainy went completely rigid when the guys mentioned Noah Drummond would be attending their little strategy session later. She wanted to ask why but knew the time wasn't right. Maybe after they'd had a few drinks, the other woman would be more open about why his name seemed to shoot electricity up her spine. She hadn't realized she'd stopped chopping until she looked up to see Collin standing close and looking at her thoughtfully.

"Sweetness, are you okay? I spoke your name twice before you came back to me."

"Oh, really? Drat, sorry for that, I was just sort of lost

in thought I guess. I missed you last night. What time did you finally come upstairs?" She turned on her seat so she could lean forward and rest her cheek against his warm chest.

"It was too late to come in and disturb you, so I just went to my room. I don't require much sleep. There will be times when I'll work through the night, so I can spend more time with you during the day while Cash and Clay are busy elsewhere." He wrapped his arms around her and kissed the top of her head, then leaned down and moved her curls aside so he could speak against her ear. "Now, people are going to start arriving soon, but I haven't had any alone time with you yet. Do you feel up to a bit of play before your party?"

Yep, panty-soaking moment.

Feeling his warm breath against her ear was enough to make her pussy flood with cream. "Yes, please," was all she managed to squeak out before he'd scooped her up and started down the stairs.

"I'm going to make a huge exception to my own rule about you being naked before you enter the playroom for two reasons. First, I'm not sure I can wait long enough for us to juggle around those casts out here in the hall. And second, the sooner you are settled on the table, the sooner I can fuck you." He chuckled at her gasp as they made their way into the dark playroom. He had her clothes stripped off in seconds, and he was securing her to the large padded table they'd used before.

"I'm going to strap you on to the table, sweetness, I want you safe." He grinned at her, and for just a second, she got a glimpse of the ornery boy she was sure he'd been. "I'm not sure you can handle another accident just now."

Haha, everybody's a comedian.

She just smiled and nodded, no sense messing up the promise of sex by giving voice to her sarcasm. Besides, getting sassy with a Dom hadn't proven to be a particularly wise choice previously. Layla gave herself a mental high-five for learning, albeit slowly, how to play this game.

"You're very wet for me aren't you, sweet sub?" Collin asked, drawing his fingers through her wet folds. "That makes me very happy. Let's see if I can't come up with a reward for you."

She heard him open a drawer below her, but she was quickly losing focus on anything but his fingers trailing from her rear hole to just shy of her clit. When she tried to tilt her hips to force his fingers that last bit further, she nearly growled with frustration.

"All in good time, sweetness," he chuckled.

She could feel her entire body flushing with desire, and her breathing was little more than panting. Holy shit, the things he could do with his fingers was enough to make her go insane.

"Talk to me, Layla, I want to hear your voice. We are in this room mostly because I wanted access to the—shall we say accessories? Unless you are specifically told to keep quiet, it is my pleasure to hear every soft sigh and sweet moan. I relish each whisper, and I'll spend the rest of my life making sure your needs are not just met but exceeded. I'll cherish you—body and soul—if you'll let me, pet."

Without warning, his lips locked over her clit, he sucked it between his teeth, and she felt her body come completely apart. It was as if she had gone from near zero to Mach one in a fraction of a second. The intensity of the orgasm caused her to scream, then chant Collin's name until she was barely able to rasp out a sound.

When she finally managed to open her eyes, he had

spread her legs wide, still strapped to the wings of the table, allowing him to step right up against her still pulsing pussy. He was sliding the head of his cock through the wet folds of her labia, smiling at her.

"You are so fucking beautiful, and when you come, you literally glow from the inside out—it's a radiance that wraps itself around my heart and fills my soul with light. You are a gift straight from the Great Spirit. I'm going to sink into you and take you right back up to the top again."

Layla felt each bump and ridge of his cock as he slid into her swollen channel, and every inch was pure bliss. She tried to keep her eyes open and locked on his, but the feeling was so incredible, she realized her eyes had rolled back, and her head was tilted back so far, the only thing he'd be able to see was the bottom of her chin. She forced herself to find his gaze again and nearly came when she saw love and lust vying for supremacy in his dark eyes.

"Oh my God, you feel so unbelievably good inside me. Your cock is velvet over hot steel, and it's so... oh, so huge... it fills me so full and pushes in so far, I can feel every glorious ridge caressing me."

He started with long, slow strokes but finally picked up the pace, and she lost any hope of coherent speech. When he tilted his hips, so he slid over her G-spot, it was as if he'd launched them both into space. She felt her muscles quiver, then clamp down with an intensity she didn't know she possessed a heartbeat before she screamed as the joy of their combined release assailed her. It was made all the more intense by the feel of his cock pulsing deep inside her.

Layla was still basking in the afterglow when she felt Collin wiping off her sex with a warm damp cloth. When she reached for it, he laid his hand on her lower abdomen.

"Be still, I love taking care of you. Please don't deny

me the honor." He carried her into the bathroom and helped her freshen up and get redressed before taking her into the beach room. He settled her in one of the lounge chairs, elevating her ankle. She watched as he picked up a remote, and suddenly, the room was filled with the sounds of the ocean and the faint sound of Caribbean music.

"Oh, it's so perfect," she laughed. "It sounds as if I'm sitting outside a real beachside bar. You are brilliant and so sweet. I don't think I told you the other night how much this room means to me. It's amazing and the fact you listened to me and *remembered*… well, it touches my heart… I want you to know that."

He leaned down and kissed her with an intensity that surprised her, considering they had both just had "shake me to my core" orgasms. When he pulled back, he smiled and brushed his finger down her nose.

"Eventually, you're going to understand just how important you are, sweetheart. But until then, we plan to keep reminding you. Now, I want you to lie back and rest a bit before your guests arrive."

"But I need to help Ilaina with the rest of the food. It's not fair to expect her to do all the work."

"You're kidding, right? She is in seventh heaven up there, bossing around two of her brothers. Now, be a good girl and catch a few minutes' rest before the wild women of ShadowDance Mountain descend upon you." He covered her with a soft throw and dimmed the lights a bit before he left.

Her last thoughts as she drifted off were about being the luckiest woman alive.

NICK LANG SAT down the road from Red Clouds Dancing and watched as a half dozen trucks made their way past the new business to head down the lane leading to the men's home. He had to laugh, some special ops agents these jokers were. Not a single one of the drivers had even given him a second glance. He'd planned to check out their house tonight, but now it looked like that was going to have to wait.

He'd hit their little dancehall and find himself a distraction later. Hell, it was almost the weekend, there ought to be at least a few women to pick from. Not that he was overly particular after having been *mostly* celibate while in prison. There had been women willing to fuck the inmates, hell, there had been male staff willing to provide services as well. Never let it be said prisons weren't subject to all the same temptations as the streets—the economy was just greatly exaggerated.

His research had yielded some interesting information about the Red Clouds, and it appeared the brothers were an interesting group. Hell, the middle one was a rich bastard. Maybe he should just kidnap Layla and collect a few million before he sliced her up. He'd give her back alright—every piece. He laughed at his own joke and settled in to wait. It would be a few hours before the dance club was hopping, no need to be seen driving all over town and risk being noticed. No, he'd just kick back and rest a bit, no need to tempt fate.

ALEX ESCORTED KAT through the front door of the Red Clouds' home and watched as his brother and Jamie Creed disappeared into the trees along the creek. Kat looked up at him and frowned.

"Did you see that? They just fuc… um, I mean they just disappeared. Did you guys have to take a class in that or something?" She smiled at Alex sweetly but judging by his frown, it hadn't been the distraction she'd hoped for. Damn, she really was losing her touch lately.

He leaned down and whispered in her ear, "Close, but not close enough, my love," and gave her a sharp swat. Okay, so maybe this evening had some potential for later after all. Neither Alex nor Zach had seemed interested in punishing her for anything recently, and she had even made an effort—more than once—to push them. Kat tried to look contrite but wasn't sure she'd pulled it off.

"Come on, girlfriend, before you get yourself in more trouble than you can handle. Cash says we should head on downstairs and follow the music. That sounds like it has potential, so let's get a move on." Tori Bartell was dragging her down the hall before she'd even gotten a kiss, damn it anyway.

"Okay, but I just got cheated out of a kiss, I'll have you know. Damn, who lit a fire under your ass, anyway?"

"Hush, I have to pee again, and if Trace sees me, he's going to be on me like white on rice." She glanced around quickly and asked, "Is Mitch going to be here?" When Kat nodded, Tori cursed a blue streak as they made their way down the stairs. "Shit, you have to promise to keep him away from me."

Kat dug her heels in the minute they got near the door. "Why?"

Tori sighed and pulled her into the room. *"We're here. Finally.* Sorry, but we had to wait for Kat to get her ass swatted before coming downstairs. You know how greedy she is."

The other women giggled, and Kat just rolled her eyes. Jenna was already reclining on a lounge chair with a large glass of what looked like orange juice with fruit in it. Her sweet friend and sister-in-law was due any minute, and the little "warrior fairy," as her brothers liked to call her, looked like she had an extra-large beach ball stuffed under her shirt. She also seemed stressed, and Kat made a mental note to find out what that was about… as soon as she got her drink.

Looking around the beach room, Kat was impressed with what the Red Clouds had created. Cash had asked both her and Tori for input, so she'd known they were making it, but damn, they'd outdone themselves. *One thing about Doms, there isn't much they won't do for the right sub.*

Turning she came face to face with Bree. "Hey there, how are you? I haven't seen you out of that flippin' hospital since you got back."

"I know," the pretty woman laughed and nodded. "I've been trying to give Doc some time off after he was nice enough to let me take vacation time for a honeymoon so soon after joining the staff. I was just heading over to check on Jenna, she looks a bit pale."

Sitting down next to Jenna, Kat watched as Bree asked her a number of questions and didn't seem satisfied with any of the answers. Kat leaned forward and asked, "You want me to get Colt, Jenna?" Just then, Rissa leaned down to see what was going on while Ilaina and Tori were trying to keep Layla from hopping over to them on one leg.

Jenna smiled and just shook her head. "I'd like to wait a few minutes if you think it's okay. I really think it's just indigestion again. I've had it on and off since last night. I've taken antacids, but they don't seem to be helping. Seems little Daniel is a handful already." She was rubbing slow circles over her rounded tummy as if she could coax the little guy into cooperating.

Kat announced she needed another drink and headed for the bar. While Bree continued to talk to Jenna, Kat sent a quick text to Alex, and despite her request that they *casually* make their way downstairs, it sounded like a herd of elephants was stampeding toward them. Sighing to herself, she knew Jenna was going to know she'd ratted her out.

"Shit! Kat, you are a rat-fink. Don't think I don't know what you've done. Crap."

"Damn and double damn, I told Alex to be subtle. I swear the man doesn't know subtle from fu...ric-rac." She amended her words just in the nick of time, and Tori leaned over to give her a high-five.

"Well done, girlfriend. I'm not sure I've ever heard that expression before, but you get points for creativity and thinking on your feet, that's for sure!"

Alex frowned at her but then refocused his attention on his sister. Leaning over, he whispered, "I'll deal with you later, my lovely wife." But he didn't seem all that committed to the idea if you asked Kat. Sighing, she knew all hope for a nice session in the playroom had just been torched by her soon to be born nephew. *I'm going to have a chat with you about this nonsense young man.*

Kat moved to the back of the room and let everyone

discuss what should be done. They all agreed to take Jenna to the hospital so she could be checked, and Bree was going along despite having just come off a fourteen-hour shift. Kat watched as Ethan frowned but agreed to go along as well. Moving to Jenna's side, she gave her a quick hug and promised she'd come right away if they kept her. She also assured her friend she'd bring her bag.

Trying to behave as she ordinarily did was exhausting when she felt anything but normal. She was once again feeling disconnected and in general just off her game, just like so many other times since she'd had the triplets. She couldn't seem to nail down what it was she was feeling. Both Alex and Zach had been unusually distant, and she was starting to worry. It wasn't as if their past wasn't already littered with challenges, but now she feared maybe they truly had lost interest in her.

Alex offered to drive Colt's truck so he could hold his wife in the back as they made their way the short distance to the hospital. He turned to her.

"Wait for Zach, he can bring you if and when he's ready." Then he'd turned and stalked away. She'd barely managed to contain her tears until she was able to rush past several of her friends and make her way into the tiny bathroom.

Chapter 20

L AYLA HAD WATCHED the scene play out and worried about her sweet friends. One was being spirited away to the hospital, and the concerned look on Bree's face had everyone unsettled. Then Alex's abrupt treatment of the woman he was known to adore was completely baffling and had clearly upset Kat tremendously.

Looking around, Layla noticed Mitch Grayson had been one of the people Kat brushed against in her haste to escape before she'd succumbed to the hurt Layla had seen in her eyes. Layla had been told Mitch was a strong empath, and he'd clearly gotten something from his encounter with Kat. He was clearly disturbed by whatever he'd sensed from Katarina, but he was also trying desperately to distract his wife who was currently badgering him for information.

"Rissa, baby, please. I'll talk to you about this in a bit. Right now, let's focus on the other more pressing issues at hand. We've got to wait for Jamie and Zach's report, then we'll decide how to proceed. No matter how this plays out, I'll be taking you back home. Bryant and Betsy need you there more than you need to be at the hospital. Now, go check on your friend and meet me back upstairs in five— please." Layla smiled as he kissed his wife on the nose and turned her toward the bathroom.

As he walked by, Mitch knelt beside her. Smiling, he took her hand in his, "Don't worry so much, Layla. You are in great hands. Your men are going to take excellent care of you, they love you very much. You have the whole ShadowDance team behind you as well. Just so you know, your uncle was sitting down the road when we all drove by. He thinks we didn't notice, that we're all a bunch of hicks." When she started to protest, he put his hand up.

"No, leave it, please. That is exactly how we like things—if he underestimates us, it'll make our job a lot easier. He'll make a mistake quicker, and we'll be able to snatch him up. Although we'd have to lock him up quickly because if Cash gets his hands on him, the asshat is a dead man." Mitch smiled and shook his head. "And just to put your mind at ease, the thing with Alex and Kat is not at all what it appears to be, and I'm going to be chatting with my friend in just a few minutes about that. He is so focused on his own agenda, he has forgotten the sensitive woman he's doing it all for."

Layla wasn't sure what to make of Mitch Grayson. From the things she'd heard, his gifts were almost frightening in their intensity. Yet the few times she'd personally spoken with her, she'd noticed he was amazingly sensitive and considerate in the way he approached people with information.

Before he walked out the door, he turned and walked back to her one last time, leaning down to whisper in her ear. "I won't tell your men, but you need to as quickly as possible." She must have looked as puzzled as she felt because he laughed and added, "Let's just say this, shall we? No more of those pain pills and no liquor either, little mama." With those words, he was gone, and Layla was left gasping for breath.

How could it be? She'd been tracking her cycle for years because she had never felt comfortable filling her body with the hormones of birth control pills and… *oh shit.* She just now realized she hadn't paid any attention to any of this since the moment she'd met the Red Cloud brothers.

The thought of being pregnant both thrilled and terrified her. What would the men think? They had alluded to their relationship being permanent, but none of them had counted on this. The last thing she wanted was for them to feel obligated to marry her, and now, they were being forced to deal with her past as well. *Oh, you're a real catch, Layla… yes indeed… a crazy-ass murdering piece of shit uncle and knocked up… every man's dream woman.*

Coming back to the present, she realized she had not only spoken the words out loud, but she wasn't alone either. *Fuck! Honestly, could you screw this day up any worse?* Taking a deep breath, Layla decided it was time to turn around and find out who was standing behind her. She let out a sigh of pure relief to see Tori, Kat, Rissa, and Ilaina smiling at her. *At least it wasn't one of the guys.*

"Don't suppose there's any way you didn't hear that, is there?"

Tori squealed and leaned down to pull her into a hug so tight, Layla heard herself squeak. "Oh Lord love a leper, this is so amazing. We're going to be doing this together, I'm pregnant, too. Trace doesn't know yet, I've had this super romantic dinner planned for a week now." Pausing to look around when they all giggled, she frowned.

"Hey, knock that shit off… of course, I'm not cooking. I told you, I've been planning a romantic dinner, and that doesn't involve the local fire department." She sighed deeply and added, "Besides, Fire Chief McAllister made me promise I wouldn't cook again until after he retires, the ornery old fart." She giggled, the sound so contagious, Layla found herself snickering as well.

"Chief McAllister was so funny the last time his crew had to come to the office because I'd tried to make my own lunch in the break room. He said, 'Honey, if'n you'll stop with this cooking business, I promise to buy your lunch every day until I retire.' He's such a sweetie, but God Almighty, it was embarrassing." By the time she'd finished, all the women were laughing almost hysterically because her imitation of the elderly chief of the small Climax Fire Department had been nearly perfect.

Suddenly, Layla was almost overwhelmed with her appreciation for her new friends and particularly for Tori. Her sweet pal had known how close to the edge Layla had been and had defused the emotion with another of her cooking disaster stories. Looking at the small group of women surrounding her, she found herself focused on Ilaina.

"Please don't tell your brothers about this. I need a little time to absorb and confirm it. I know I've felt off for a while, but I really did attribute it to stress. I promise I won't do anything crazy, but I really do need to process everything first."

Ilaina leaned forward and hugged her. "I understand, and I'll keep your secret for a while, but I won't be able to contain my excitement forever, I'm just warning you. Oh—and you'd do well to avoid Granny Good-Witch like the plague. She'll out you in a heartbeat, and trust me, she'll know the minute you walk in the room. That old woman doesn't miss a thing, and Cash is her darling—hell, you'd think he had personally hung the sun and the moon—so she'll go nine-one-one on this in a heartbeat."

She must have realized they were all staring at her because she looked around and added, "What?"

Kat spoke up first, "Well, damn and double damn, it's good to know that one of the world's most famous faces is still attached to a mouthy sister. Welcome home, Lainy."

There was another round of giggles before they all headed upstairs to find out what the men had learned about Nick Lang and if there had been any news about Jenna. Layla was proud of how quickly she'd mastered the crutches, but stairs were a challenge, so her friends had surrounded her and helped. They were all giggling like school girls by the time they topped the long stairway.

Several hours later, they stood at the glass in the Climax Hospital's nursery and looked on as Daniel Matthews slept peacefully in his small glass bassinette. His dark hair and golden tan skin were a gift from his mother's Native American heritage, but his sweet face and size were definitely from his doting daddy. When Layla looked over at Kat, she noted the tears in the other woman's eyes. Kat smiled without ever taking her eyes off the baby.

"He's so perfect, and I'm going to be the best aunt ever, you just wait and see. God, I can't wait to hold him in my arms and cuddle him. I miss the cuddling. My three terrors don't want to hold still until they collapse from exhaustion... oh wait, that's me who collapses." She smiled wanly and turned to look at Layla. "You and Tori are going to be amazing mothers, and you've got lots of help if you need it, don't forget that, okay?"

Layla could only nod her head in agreement because she was so close to tears, she didn't dare speak. Damn, she hoped she wasn't going to be one of those cry-baby pregnant women, then she had to suppress a giggle. It seemed she was going to be one of those psycho-pregnant women that talked to themselves instead. *Geez, Layla... get a fucking grip already.*

As they made their way to Jenna's room, Layla noticed Mitch standing in an alcove, and he appeared to be having a very heated discussion with both of her bosses. Layla managed to distract Kat by pretending to struggle with her crutches, so she missed the scene unfolding just a few feet away, and they breezed into the new mama's room without incident.

Jenna's C-section hadn't been planned, but from what Layla had heard, Bree had tugged little Daniel into the world in short order when it had been apparent he was in distress. Jenna looked up and smiled at them, obviously feeling the effects of the pain medications she'd been given.

"Did you see him? He's so perfect. I want to hold him, but everybody keeps whining about me resting."

Kat rushed over to the side of the bed and assured her sister-in-law she'd have her sweet bundle in here in no time. "Sweet sister mine, of course, my nephew is perfect. He's brilliant, too, after all, look who he picked as an aunt." Jenna had already settled back against the pillows and was asleep as Kat stroked the side of her face before she added, "Even if I'm not his uncles' favorite person anymore, I'll always love him like one of my own."

Layla was sure Kat had forgotten Colt stood in the corner listening, and neither of them had noticed Alex and Zach until Alex spoke.

"Katarina, Zach and I would like to speak with you. Let's go, love. You can return later when our sweet sister has had a chance to rest up a bit."

Layla sensed a hesitance in Kat she'd never seen before, and it unsettled her. It was obvious both men were tense, and Layla couldn't help but worry about her new friend.

Making her way back to the waiting room, Layla was shocked to see it filled to overflowing with well-wishers. Blue flowers and balloons topped every table, and there was a rush of people asking her if she'd seen the baby. When she explained he was in the nursery, she'd nearly been stampeded as women rushed from the room.

As the crowd began to thin, a distinguished looking man and beautiful woman, she assumed were Daniel and Catherine Lamont, breezed through the doors, and Layla almost laughed out loud watching Daniel's long legs eating up the hallway with his wife scrambling to keep up. Despite his rushed pace, he stopped at the nurse's station.

"Good evening, I'm Daniel Lamont, and this lovely woman is my wife, Catherine. We'd like to see our daughter, Jenna Matthews, and our new grandson. If you'd direct us to her room, I'd certainly appreciate it."

Layla almost choked as every nurse within earshot moved to help the charming man. *Easy to see why everyone speaks so highly of the elder Lamonts, that's for sure.* As she watched them move down the hall, Layla suddenly realized there wasn't anyone in the large, open room that she recognized.

A sudden chill raced up her spine as she took in her surroundings. The only person she saw who seemed out of place was a shadowy figure standing partially hidden by a door frame at the other end of the hall. She glanced toward the sliding glass doors leading outside, and when she looked again, he was gone.

Her heart was racing, and Layla felt herself sliding into panic. He was here, she just knew it, but now it wasn't just about her anymore, she had to keep her child safe. Intending to make her way back down the hall so she wouldn't feel so alone, she dropped her crutches and wrapped her arms around her waist. When she tried to turn on her heel, she fell right into Cash's arms. She would have landed on her ass if he hadn't caught her.

"Love, where have you been? We've been searching for you." All three of them were standing around her in a tight circle, and it was easy to see they'd been worried.

"What? Oh, Kat and I went down the hall to see baby Daniel in the nursery. Kat is struggling today, and I didn't want her to be alone." She looked up and saw indulgence in all three of their eyes. "I'm sorry, I didn't realize it had taken so long.

"Um... did you just see a strange man standing down there?" She gestured down the hall, and Clay took off running in that direction. Cash and Collin moved so quickly, they were little more than a blur as Collin grabbed her crutches and Cash picked her up into his arms and rushed out the doors to their truck. They didn't wait for Clay, explaining they preferred to get her home and safe first.

"That's why we were so worried, sweetheart. Jamie and Zach managed to get close enough to Nick's car to put a tracker on it, so we knew he was parked just down the street." Collin had taken her hand in his and was working gently to unclench her fists. She hadn't even realized she'd balled her hands into tense fists until she felt him massaging the aching digits.

CASH HAD NEARLY wrecked the place looking for her and still didn't understand how they'd missed finding Layla during their frantic search. Christ, the damned hospital wasn't *that* large, and she was on crutches for fuck's sake. How had they all forgotten the viewing area in the nursery?

As he wheeled into the driveway, he parked as close to their front door as possible. Collin carried her into the house, then caught the keys Cash tossed him. Collin quickly kissed Layla goodbye and ran back out the door.

Looking over at Layla as she leaned on those blasted crutches, Cash noted the dark circles under her eyes and was suddenly aware that, for a group of Doms, they were doing a mighty poor job of caring for their woman.

"Come on, love. Let's get you settled. Hang on to my shoulders while I set these aside." He moved the crutches and picked her up, cradling her in his arms. He loved how perfectly she fit against him. Sitting on the sofa, he just held her on his lap for a while, satisfaction spreading through him. It was peaceful, and she was obviously enjoying the moment because she'd snuggled against him and promptly fallen asleep.

Thinking back, he realized she'd been tired a lot lately and vowed to make sure she took better care of herself. She was obviously struggling to keep up with her job and three men, not to mention the extra effort it took to do everything with two damned casts and crutches. Hell, the one time he'd had to use crutches when he'd been in high school, he'd thought they were the most exhausting things he'd ever dealt with.

Leaning back so he could look down into her sweet face, he was suddenly struck by how different his life was now. His sweet grandmother had said when he found "the one," his entire worldview would shift. He had smiled and nodded affectionately at her but hadn't really taken the words to heart. It was crystal clear now how right she'd been. Brushing his fingers down the side of Layla's face, he smiled when she pushed closer and leaned into his touch.

How many hellholes around the world had he lain in, night after night, wondering if she was out there some-where—needing him and he wasn't there. Did she wonder what was taking him so long? Had the woman he'd only dreamed existed given up on him walking into her life? Or was she still waiting—fighting the trials all alone?

Cash shook his head at what, at the time, had seemed like delusional dreaming, but now seemed to have been more prophetic than he could have known. From the dates he'd seen on the reports Mitch had forwarded to them, Layla would have been dealing with every imaginable difficulty at the same time he had been experiencing the haunting dreams and asking himself those difficult questions.

Grandmother told me the power of love binds souls together before they are ever born, so I don't know why I'm surprised—but I am—hell, I'm totally blown away. There was something different about Layla now, and he couldn't identify what exactly it was, but it was there—niggling at the back of his mind.

Chapter 21

C LAY THOROUGHLY SEARCHED the entire corridor and came up empty. When Collin called from the parking lot, he made his way out, and they were on their way home in minutes. He wasn't surprised he couldn't find Nick Lang but figured it was worth a shot.

Mitch had stopped him as he'd left and cautioned him that Layla was in desperate need of reassurance and rest. What the fuck had that meant, anyway. Christ, special ops guys talked in riddles. Cowboys were usually just in-your-face-blunt most of the time, but at least you understood what they were saying. Sure, they were often abrasive and rude, and occasionally, their trash talk started fights, but at least you didn't have to unscramble the damned message.

Relaying the cryptic comment to Collin on the way home, Clay saw his brother was as confused as he'd been. Walking in the front door, the first thing Clay noticed was Cash sitting with Layla fast asleep in his lap. When he approached, he smiled down at how small she looked in his arms.

"God, she is so beautiful—sometimes, I have to remind myself she's real. Honestly, it's like the three of us sent our individual wishes to heaven, and they made her just for us."

When Cash asked where Lainy was, both he and Collin

looked at each other and shrugged. "I didn't see her at the hospital. Did you call her cell?"

Just then the front door slammed, and Lainy stormed past them muttering to herself about "lame assed brothers" and "leaving me stranded" and something about Noah Drummond and dinner. Before they could question her, she disappeared down the hall, the door to her apartment slammed, and the lock engaged with a loud click.

"Holy shit. Were we supposed to bring her home? I didn't even see her after we left here. Damn, Collin and I were never her favorite people, to begin with, this sucks." Clay stuck his hands in the pockets of his jacket and felt the small sack Bree had given him as he'd left the waiting room. "Oh, here, Bree gave this to me for Layla. She said something about Tori telling her our great news and to have Layla take these until she can make an appointment next week." When both Cash and Collin looked up at him, he shrugged.

"Hey, I'm just a cowboy. I didn't ask any questions." Then he grinned, placed his hand over his heart before reciting with great dramatic flair, "Mine is not to question why, mine is but to do or die."

"Christ, spare us." Collin rolled his eyes and grabbed the small bag. "Probably more meds, but what's the good news?" Opening the small bag to remove the contents, he held the small bottle in his hand and stared at it before plopping down in the closest chair.

"Holy shit."

Clay moved quickly to grab the small bottle and gulped.

"Wow."

LAYLA HAD BEEN sleeping so peacefully in Cash's arms. He'd propped up both her casts, pulled a throw around her, and the steady beat of his heart had lulled her right back to sleep. When a door slammed down the hall, she started to surface but decided she was just too comfy to give it up just yet.

Then she heard Clay's comments about the good news and the bottle. Drat, she was *so* busted. Damn small towns, she could see now, this was going to be a major pain in the ass. Neither Collin nor Clay had sounded happy to see what she was fairly certain were prenatal vitamins. Fracking fairy farts, how was she going to get out of this one?

She knew when Cash saw what Clay had set on the table because his heart skipped a beat... or three, and the air whooshed out of his lungs. He immediately tightened his arms around her in a move that could have only been described as protective, and that gave her a glimmer of hope she might not completely sink alone on this one.

"Layla, love, I know you are awake because I swear I can hear you thinking. Care to enlighten us?" She thought about continuing to pretend she was sleeping... she really did, but in the end, it seemed cowardly and would probably only buy her a couple of extra minutes, anyway. Taking a deep breath, she opened her eyes and tried to slide off Cash's lap.

"No, love, stay right where you are."

She was worried they were going to be angry or worse, think she'd done this on purpose in an attempt to entrap them, but she hoped those fears weren't written all over her face.

"Let's start with how long you have known, shall we?"

Oh boy, he sounded pissed. She hadn't ever seen him angry, at least not at her, and that unsettled her even more.

"Well, I didn't actually know, well, not until Mitch said something before we all went to the hospital to see Jenna." She was playing with the hem of her shirt, afraid to look up into their eyes. What if they didn't want anything to do with her or the baby? What if she had to move again and start over? It had been a scary thought before she'd found out, but it was downright terrifying now. "I'm so sorry." Cash pulled her back and looked at her as if she'd suddenly sprouted a second head.

"What did you say?"

"I said I'm sorry. I really didn't do this on purpose, I swear." She tried again to get off of his lap because she needed distance. "Please, let me up. I really need to... um, well, I need to be able to see you all and, well..." She felt the tears spill over. "Damn, I hate crying, it makes me feel helpless, and I hate that more than anything."

"That distance you're trying to establish, sweet sub, is exactly why Cash isn't letting you off his lap, and if he does, Clay or I will be pulling your sweet ass onto ours." Collin's words surprised her, and he must have read that in her eyes. "Did you really think we wouldn't be absolutely over the moon about this?" She jerked her eyes from him to Clay, then up to Cash.

"Um, well, I didn't know. We really hadn't discussed anything permanent, and we sure hadn't discussed children." Of course, her stomach chose that particular moment to growl so loudly, all three men looked at her stomach and laughed. "Oh dear, that's kind of embarrassing. I seem to be hungry all the time, and well, at least this explains why I've been so tired lately. I was afraid I was getting lazy, and damn if I don't hate lazy even more than crying... are you sure you aren't mad? I don't want any money from you, really. And I'll let you spend all the time you want with the baby, well, if I don't have to find another job someplace else. Do you think the Lamonts will let me stay working for them when they find out? I don't want them to look bad in the community by employing me or anything. I know my mom always warned me if I got 'knocked up,' I wouldn't be able to have a job because no one would want an unmarried pregnant woman waddling around. And I—" Cash had stopped her by placing his finger over her lips and shaking his head.

"That's enough. If I ever get my hands on your mother, I'm not going to be responsible for my actions. Your marital status will not mean diddly squat to Alex or Zach— and as I recall, you have a lease to own contract, anyway. Now, as for us not being happy about the baby, well, you couldn't possibly be any more off the mark. The *only thing* this changes is how quickly we propose, something that was already well in the works, I assure you. And if you'll stop and think, you'll realize we have indeed been dropping hints by the truck-load that we all want you forever. As remarkable as it seems, we have obviously been too subtle." He finally smiled, and she felt herself relax a bit as she absorbed his words. "Now, let's get you something to eat because you, sweet mama, need to start taking better care of yourself."

He stood up with her still in his arms as if she didn't weigh a thing and kissed her on the forehead before handing her over to Clay. They were nearly to the kitchen when there was a knock at the front door, and as Collin turned that way, Ilaina came storming down the hall toward the door. She stopped in front of Collin and started tapping her beautiful nails against his chest.

"Some genius you are, big brother. I hope Layla doesn't ever send you to town with the baby, you're liable to leave the poor child God only knows where. I seriously can't believe you forgot me." Layla watched as a look of sheer vulnerability and sadness passed over her stunning face before she was able to quickly mask it. "Now, because of you three ass hats, I have... I have to go to dinner with Noah Drummond. Do you know how difficult... oh, balls... never mind?"

Layla watched as Lainy walked away and marveled at how effortlessly she managed those four-inch stilettos. Layla had never been very graceful in heels, but it hadn't mattered because she hadn't ever had the money to buy pretty shoes, anyway. It suddenly occurred to her that her baby was going to have Ilaina for an aunt. When she giggled, Clay looked down at her and raised an eyebrow in question. She shook her head before answering.

"I was just thinking about how amazing it is the baby is going to have the world-famous Ilaina for an aunt, then it occurred to me that he or she is going to have three daddies, and that probably trumps a famous aunt. Mercy, are you sure you want to keep me, I think I'm sort of skating on the edge of sanity lately." Clay looked at her and smiled.

"Never even been in question, baby."

ILAINA OPENED THE front door to find Noah smiling at her with a cat-that-swallowed-the-canary look. No, scratch that, it was more like a cat that had the canary cornered and planned to play with it before eating it look.

Joy, joy, she was walking right into the lion's den and would probably end up pulling its tail before all was said and done. What she didn't understand was why this man unnerved her so. She'd dealt with men all over the world, met kings and sultans without breaking a sweat. So, why did this man make her feel like an inept teenager? They'd been friends at one time... but then one night of poor decisions had changed everything. They'd become oil and water, and Noah just seemed to keep on mixing.

"*Cara*, you look lovely. Are you ready for a fun dinner?" Noah's deep voice had always reminded her of a smooth whiskey—sweet right before it burned you.

"Look, Noah, you and I both know there is too much"—she took a deep breath and let it out before continuing—"history between us for this to ever work. How about we just agree to be friends?" Truthfully, she didn't think that would ever work either, but she still felt like she should extend the olive branch.

"Let's see how this goes, what do you say?" Escorting her to his truck, he opened the door and lifted her onto her seat. When they'd made the way down the long drive, he didn't turn into the parking lot of Red Clouds Dancing. When she looked at him in question, he just smiled.

"*Cara*, I asked you to dinner, but I didn't say *where* we'd be eating. I have something to show you first."

They rode the rest of the way in silence, and she was surprised when he stopped in front of what had been an old mill when they'd been kids.

"Why are we here, Noah? Do you have permission for us to be here?"

"I do." Just as he started to open his door, his phone

rang. She saw him grimace when he looked at the screen, but he settled back in his seat and answered. "Alex, what can I do for you?"

Ilaina was surprised to hear him speaking with a man she assumed was Alex Lamont. Noah Drummond was an enigma that was for sure. What possible connection could there be between a photographer and men she knew still dealt with what her oldest brother called black ops. She finally decided to stop pretending she wasn't listening when he took her hand and pulled it up to kiss the palm.

"I am getting ready to have dinner with Ilaina, then I'll come up, and we'll talk. I'm not making any promises beyond that."

She wasn't sure exactly what was happening, but one thing was clear, he was not pleased with the turn of events. It wasn't that she knew him that well anymore, but she'd learned to read people's body language over the years, and his was filled with stress that hadn't been there before the call.

"*Cara*, I'm sorry we'll have to skip the tour for now. I was so looking forward to sharing something with you, but that call was from a mutual friend of ours, Alex Lamont. I promise you, I would not have cut this evening short for anything short of a major emergency." He started his truck, and as he drove, he finally said, "I can't tell you everything about this because it isn't really my story to tell, but I want you to know, it involves a child who holds a special place in the hearts of Alex's team. If there is a way for me to help, I must."

For the first time, she saw a glimpse of the man Noah Drummond had become, and she was genuinely surprised to discover she liked that man a lot.

"You know, Noah, I think you and I will be good

friends again after all. Thank you for allowing me to see a bit of who you are now." She smiled at him and found herself looking forward to the dinner more than she would have ever imagined possible.

Lainy thoroughly enjoyed her time with Noah. They'd driven to a small neighboring town and eaten at a quaint little steakhouse with gingham-covered tables set out along a fast running mountain stream. Looking down into the crystal-clear water from the snow melt up the mountain, she smiled, knowing how cold that water would be despite the warm air surrounding them. They hadn't gotten the snow that had been predicted a few days earlier, and she was holding on to the hope Spring was just around the corner.

She'd known why he had wanted to get out of their hometown; one of the downsides of returning home was having everyone in town stop by your table to chat. When Noah had told her, "I want you all to myself," Lainy had known exactly what he was talking about.

The only downside of spending time alone with Noah Drummond was she was, well... *alone* with Noah Drummond. Sighing to herself, she tried to shake off her growing sense of comfort and rapport with the one man who had always been able to undo her.

Don't let your guard down so easily again, Lainy.

Chapter 22

L AYLA HAD BEEN trying to forget her uncle was still eluding apprehension, but with three men hovering over her night and day, it was impossible. It had been nearly four weeks since she'd fractured her wrist. It hadn't been broken all the way through, so Bree let her remove the cast early. Layla was now in a lace-up walking cast for her ankle and relieved beyond words she no longer had to rely on crutches.

Being mobile had never felt so good. Mia Marshall was teaching her how to use the Glock 19 Cash had insisted she carry with her at all times. He and his brothers had started asking her at odd times to prove it was on her person or within her reach, and if she didn't have it, she didn't get to come that night. Personally, she'd have rather had their threatened spankings, but they'd decided she'd like them too much.

When she'd complained about that to Tori, her friend had burst out laughing before quickly agreeing denying her an orgasm really did fall under "cruel and unusual punishment." *Proof it pays to have a best friend who was a lawyer.*

She and Tori were sitting in a small downtown diner when they saw Kat walking by and tapped on the glass to get her attention. When Kat looked up, Layla and Tori both gasped at the tear-stained face staring back at them.

They were both out of the booth and making their way outside to pull their friend inside before poor Kat realized what was happening.

"Kat, what on earth is wrong? Do Alex and Zach know you are so upset?" Tori pulled her into the booth beside her, blotting Kat's cold, tear-dampened cheeks dry with a hankie.

Kat just stared straight ahead for long moments before shaking her head.

"No, but I doubt they'd care. They have been pretty busy lately with some big, secret work project. All I know is it involves Noah Drummond and a young girl… and some woman keeps calling the house for them at all hours of the day and night, and they drop anything and everything to take her calls." Layla's heart went out to Kat because it was so clear hers was breaking apart, piece by piece.

"Listen, forget I said anything okay? I'm fine, really, and I should get home. Well, I guess I don't need to, it's not like I'm needed there since my husbands decided our children would be better off with a couple of live-in nannies. I guess I wasn't doing things quite to suit them on that front either."

Katarina looked at her hands for so long, Layla wasn't sure she was going to say more. Tori just kept her arm around Kat's shoulders and waited. Layla tried to stay quiet, but it was killing her.

"What aren't you saying, Kat? I feel like there is something really big you are holding back." Kat looked up at her with an expression that could only be described as haunted.

"What if they have decided I'm not worth the effort? I mean, they have already replaced me as a mother, and now, they don't even play with me anymore. I haven't been to The Club in months… I haven't had… well… let's just say our personal contact has been pretty limited lately. When Jenna had little Daniel, they assured me everything was fine, and they hadn't been trying to avoid me, but nothing changed. They insisted they'd just been really tied up with some big thing overseas, but I… I just don't know… and I don't know what to do to please them anymore."

It wasn't until that moment that Layla glanced up and realized who was sitting behind her two friends. Sheriff Dylan Marshall quietly got up and moved to the small counter to pay for his lunch and quickly made his way outside. Layla watched as he stalked to his truck, already dialing his phone before his door closed. Deciding it was best to keep that particular piece of information to herself, she saw him smile at her as he backed out of the stall. He obviously noticed she hadn't spoken to her friends when he'd seen her watching him.

Within seconds, the phone in Kat's purse started ringing. At first, Layla thought Kat was ignoring the calls, but soon it became apparent she was too distracted to notice the phone.

"Kat, are you going to answer your phone?" Layla tried to ask quietly, but still, the words seemed to startle her.

"Oh, I guess I'd better. It might be the nanny, she might actually need me for something." Pulling her phone from her purse, Layla watched as Kat's eyes widened and then filled with tears. "It was just a message. No worries." When Kat started to move out of the bench seat, Layla stayed her by placing her hand on her arm.

"Kat, hold up a minute. Would you be willing to help Tori and me plan my wedding and commitment ceremony? Since you have experience with these things, I could really use your input."

Katarina looked up at her, and for the first time in weeks, Layla saw a spark of life in her eyes. "Oh, yes, I'd love to help." She smiled and leaned forward before she spoke again, and Layla knew she was struggling to maintain control.

"Thank you. I really need some direction right now. I've been reeling for a while, you know? And if I say anything to my men, it will turn into some horrible upheaval, and I don't want that." Then turning to Tori, she added, "Remember right after the babies came home? I mentioned being 'blue,' and they called psychiatrists all over the country. Honestly, I thought I would die of embarrassment." Tori smiled and then giggled.

"I do remember, but you, my sweet friend, have forgotten something really important about our conversation that night." When Kat looked at her in confusion, Tori nudged her, "I told you to call me if you needed me, and you haven't done that, have you? Now, I fully expect our sweet Sheriff has alerted your men and probably mine and Layla's as well, so we'll be overrun at any moment. Before that happens, I want you to promise to share how you're feeling with Alex and Zach. I also want you to swear you'll call one of us when things start to swamp you, do you hear me, sweet sister?"

Layla watched as huge tears raced down Kat's pale cheeks, and Tori pulled her into a tight hug. Suddenly, feeling like she was a part of a family for the first time in years, Layla felt her own tears start to fall. Looking up, she saw the front door of the diner slam open and men storming into the small eatery. Cash was the first through the door, but Trace, Alex, and Zach, Collin, and Clay were right on his heels.

She couldn't help it... something about the whole scene was so ridiculous, it just struck her as funny, and the hysterical giggles she tried to hold in check bubbled to the surface. Seems they were contagious as well because Tori and Kat looked around them, then looked at her as if she'd completely lost her mind a split second before dissolving into roaring laughter.

Chapter 23

NICK LANG SAT in the back booth in the small diner and watched in amazement as his niece and her sexy friends had some sort of hug-fest in the front of the small eatery. A few minutes later, the entire diner was filled with men who looked like they'd been frantic to find the three women. Deciding this small town housed more than its share of perverts, he wasn't surprised they'd lured Layla in.

Christ, she was even more beautiful now than she'd been as a teenager—and he would have sworn to you that wasn't possible. Since he'd been coming in and out of this small town, he'd done some research and noted not only was Collin Red Cloud a permanent fixture on the Forbes list, the Lamonts were loaded as well.

Every time he was in this damned town, he had the feeling he was being watched and that unnerved him. It was time to step up his plan. If he was going to earn the respect of his family, he needed to get this wrapped up quickly. Things were coming together in Houston, and he needed to get back there. He wanted out of this damned town for a lot of reasons, not the least of which was it was fucking cold in Colorado, and he was getting tired of this shit in a big hurry. Taking a sip of his coffee, he cursed his glued-on mustache. Christ, being forced to wear a disguise was an insult and another mark against his traitorous niece.

Looking over as the men escorted the women out of the little café, he vowed to wrap this thing up quickly. He was tired of waiting for an opportunity to present itself—he was obviously going to have to create one. It wasn't as if he hadn't done that plenty of times before. Leaving more than enough money on the table, he slipped out the back entrance and made his way down the block to his car, just as he had every other time he'd eaten there. No sense in following that group out the front. It was time to get his gear and visit Climax's only motel.

DYLAN MARSHALL WAS getting mighty tired of watching Nick Lang watch Layla. Muttering under his breath, he wished the man would just make a move already. The way it was, he couldn't arrest the man for simply being in the same place she was, and if he picked him up solely on the threats he'd made via voice mail, the asshole would be back on the street within an hour. Giving Lang that sort of heads-up would make him more difficult to apprehend.

He'd been in the diner to keep an eye on the man when the women had converged. Ordinarily, he'd have let them talk, figuring Tori and Layla would help Katarina with the postpartum depression he knew her men were monitoring carefully, but with Nick Lang in the room, it had just been too dangerous to ignore. He'd made calls as soon as he'd cleared the door, then made his way to his observation point near where Lang had parked, just in case he decided to take Layla with him. Mitch had been tracking the man electronically and knew he'd been cyber-stalking not only Collin Red Cloud's financials but the Lamonts' as well. As far as Dylan was concerned that could only mean one thing—the man intended to make ransom demands before he evened the score with his niece.

Not in my town, you won't. Not with my friends—not ever.

After working for the Drug Enforcement Agency for years, Dylan decided to retire when his cover was so badly blown, he would have been confined to a desk job until the fucking end of time. Luckily, his dad was ready to retire as the sheriff in his hometown, so it had been an easy transition. When his sweet Mia reentered his life, he'd felt like everything was back on track, but it seemed the small town had become one hell of a magnet for trouble recently, and he was getting mighty fed-up being on the *reactive* rather than the *proactive* end of things.

Mia had been teasing him so much lately that his trigger finger was getting itchy, and they needed to visit the range so he could channel some of that energy—hell, maybe she was right. Personally, he'd rather just practice on the prick sauntering toward his car a half block down the street.

There was something different about the man today though. Dylan had noticed a shift in his energy when he'd seen him sitting in the back of the diner. It was as if he'd grown tired of waiting. The hair on the back of Dylan's neck stood up when he saw the man glance around before popping the back-end of the SUV that Dylan knew was a rental. Grabbing the binoculars he kept nearby, Dylan focused on the interior of the vehicle and saw a roll of duct tape and a coil of rope.

Oh yeah, the man was definitely ready for action. Grabbing his phone, he called Mitch and asked him to relay the info to everybody via secure texts. He didn't want it going out over his radio because it was likely a man like

Nick Lang would be using a scanner.

Pulling out a few seconds after Lang, he followed at a respectable distance since he could track the man via the small handheld GPS he'd been given after Jamie had tagged Lang a few weeks ago. When the man parked close to a small group of trees about a quarter mile from the motel, Dylan called Mitch for an update on the team they'd assembled. Despite the vehement objections of all three Red Clouds, this was the only plan any of them had been able to come up with to resolve this problem.

Watching as Cash pulled in front of the small motel and skirted the truck to open the door for Layla, he chuckled to himself knowing exactly what was inside that sweater and tucked in those knee-high leather boots. No doubt the woman was armed to the teeth. He snapped a picture with his dash-cam and e-mailed it to Mia. Within seconds he got a reply.

Yes, indeed, my, she's rockin' those boots. She's got three weapons on her. I helped the guys gussy her up. LOL Give me ten, and I'll fix 'em up good.

God, he loved that woman more than life itself, and their baby Nathanial was the light of both his and Mia's lives. Dylan knew his lovely wife had helped get Layla prepped and was grateful for her years of experience with the DEA and her willingness to pinch-hit when necessary.

He quickly texted her with a sultry promise for later that night, then returned his gaze to the couple engaged in a nearly obscene lip lock on the motel steps. *Get a room, you two. Damn, Cash, you know you have an audience. Better think how difficult it's going to be for your friends and brothers to run to her aid with hard-ons, buddy.*

Tapping his earbud, he relayed his concerns to Cash and chuckled when he saw his friend's lips twitch as he tried not to grin.

LAYLA WAS TOTALLY jazzed. Mia had helped Cash strap a tiny microphone under her sweater. There was another in her earring and a camera in her funky necklace. She had a gun tucked in the back of her pants, another in the kick-ass leather boots Ilaina had loaned her and a sheathed knife tucked down in the walking cast she was getting rid of tomorrow. Oh yes, indeed, she was feeling like one hell of a warrior woman. She'd told Cash and Mia she needed a tiara and a sword, and they'd thought she was kidding. *As if.*

After she surfaced from Cash's blistering kiss in front of the motel, she made her way through the lobby and into the break room behind her office. They'd cautioned her to do exactly what she did every other day because any break in routine would likely send her uncle scampering for the hills again. Damn it, this time she intended to put an end to this nonsense once and for all.

The last thing Cash had said to her before he'd backed away from her was, "You put him away once, love, and you can do it again, but... don't hesitate to shoot his rotten ass." She'd snickered because it was exactly what Mia had suggested... well, she'd actually suggested shooting in the same general location, just in the front. You had to love former agents and their take-no-prisoners-way of seeing the world. *Maybe I missed my calling?*

When she stepped out into her office, she saw her uncle sitting in front of her desk. It wasn't difficult to feign surprise even when she had been expecting him. His years in prison hadn't been good to him. He wasn't the same hunk women had flocked to when he was younger. The added weight and pale skin made him look much older than she knew he was.

"Well, well, look what we have here. A hot little cunt who has scored herself a rich boyfriend—or three. Jesus, Layla, your mama surely raised you better than that. Oh yeah, I forgot, after you sold my ass out, she kicked you to the curb, didn't she?" God, even his voice was more abrasive than she remembered, and his laughter at his own comment sent icy shivers up her spine.

"What do you want, Nick?" She wasn't going to give him the respect she knew he'd expect by using the title of *Uncle*. As far as she was concerned, she was an orphan the day her mom threw her and her clothes out into their front yard.

"You and I are gonna take a little ride. I have a car parked close by, and we'll just walk there nice and slow." When she saw he had a small pistol pointed at her chest she froze. "Once we get to the cabin I've rented, we'll make a couple of phone calls and see just exactly how anxious your fuck-buddies and pervert bosses are to get you back. Hell, if they make it worth my time, I might actually make this easier on you."

"Why would I go anywhere with you? We both know you'll kill me if I do, it won't matter how much they pay you." She knew she had to get more information from him, and so far, he'd been too cautious with his words. Tori had coached her on getting him to be as specific as possible. *Damn it, I still think Mia's advice is the best.*

Knowing everyone was watching and listening helped

boost her confidence. She gave her uncle a look that she hoped conveyed her utter disdain for everything he stood for.

"You really think you can force me to go with you? The years haven't been good to you, and quite frankly, I think I can take your ass." Oh boy, she could almost hear her men and the ShadowDance team growling. Sure, she knew she was poking the bear, but she also knew her uncle better than any of them did. He was going to have to be pushed to give her the information she wanted—typically, he was pretty damned calm and collected, he was nobody's fool either. He tilted his head and looked at her, clearly taking in the fact she was no longer the same trembling teen he'd frightened that last day in court.

"You know, I could have made you into something. You always were the smartest of the lot in our family. God knows, you're a lot smarter than your idiot mother. Where you got that fucking streak of justice, I'll never figure out. It's almost a shame I have to make an example of you."

"What the hell are you talking about? I thought you were going to try to ransom me for money? And just for the record, I think you are grossly overestimating my value around here. Hell, the Lamonts can hire another motel manager before they have dessert tonight, and the Red Cloud brothers like me enough, but I'm not the only woman around you know. Surely, you don't envision getting millions for me, it's unrealistic—flattering, but unrealistic." *And there it was, boys and girls… that telltale tic that means I've pushed him right over the line.*

"Maybe you aren't as smart as I thought. Let's go, I'm tired of waiting. I've been waiting for this for years. I'm going to make you understand the importance of family loyalty, then watch your eyes spark with the realization you're dead after I slit your pretty little throat. I love watching that moment when your victim knows there's no escaping death."

The minute he grabbed her arm and jerked her toward the door, she saw her chance.

She pretended to trip over the walking cast she didn't even really need anymore, falling to her hands and knees. Pulling the pistol from her boot, she didn't hesitate. He'd already told her he was going to kill her, and she knew he'd kill anyone who came through the door to help her.

She slid the small weapon into the splint she was wearing on her wrist while she struggled to get upright. When he jerked her to her feet, she pulled the trigger. It felt like she'd suddenly been caught in a time warp as everything seemed to take place in slow motion. She watched as the front of his shirt blossomed red, and his eyes went wide. It was the oddest feeling of separation from reality, almost as if she'd moved out of her own body to watch the scene from afar.

Layla heard herself say, "You're wrong you know. Watching that moment of realization when someone knows they are going to die by my hand is not at all satisfying. It's just sad because all you had to do was leave me alone." She heard his gun hit the floor at the same time his knees folded out from under him, and her small office flooded with people.

She'd known they were close but seeing them was all it took for her to deflate. Cash wrapped her in his arms, and Dylan took her weapon. Cash had her in his arms and was making his way out to the lobby in the time it took her to blink.

"I'm so proud of you, love. I'm want to spank your ass for pushing him, but damn, I'm proud of you."

Chapter 24

I T HAD TAKEN every ounce of self-control Cash had possessed to let Layla finish what she had started with her uncle. He might not have been able to restrain himself if Mia hadn't grabbed him by the arm.

"Let her do it. She's ready, and she deserves this. He took so much from her. Don't you dare deny her this moment." He'd known she was right, but it hadn't helped as much as it should have. He'd driven next door to park in the Red Clouds Dancing lot and waited. As soon as he'd been told Nick had gone in the back of the motel, he'd made his way to where Mia was positioned. She had her rifle trained on the back door and sensed his presence like the professional she was.

He knew Ethan Jantz was in position watching the front, and Jamie Creed had Lang's vehicle covered. Cash had shaken his head at the firepower awaiting the man if he stepped outside with Layla. Ethan and Jamie had been legendary as SEAL snipers—the shots they'd made would be talked about for years to come. Unfortunately, most of them were so highly classified, few people would ever get to hear those stories.

Mitch and Colt were manning all the communication from the Crow's Nest at The Club, and every single member of the team had heard firsthand how brave his woman had played the altercation with her uncle. Collin and Clay were helping the local deputies keep traffic from the area, and a couple of Dylan's deputies had been waiting outside the small cabin they'd discovered Nick Lang rented several weeks earlier. Those two deputies were the last line of defense on the off chance the man eluded everyone else. The team had put this plan together weeks ago, and for once, everything had gone like clockwork.

Remarkably, as the EMS crew wheeled Lang out, he managed to open his eyes and look straight at Layla. It had been haunting, and Cash had no doubt he'd just seen another glimpse of Satan. During all his time in the military, he'd seen that look a few times, and it always gave him chills. Most of the time he dealt with soldiers like himself who believed in their cause and were doing what they had to do, but on a few occasions, he'd seen just how real evil could be, and it had always sent a shudder up his spine.

Cuddling Layla close, he wasn't that surprised she wasn't talking. He and Zach had talked to Bree in advance and agreed they wanted to avoid giving her a sedative unless it was absolutely necessary because they didn't want to expose the baby to the medication. When he and his brothers had mentioned it to her, she had assured them she would be fine and protecting the baby was more important than making her more comfortable. Cash had asked his brothers to make sure their parents were here tomorrow night for the surprise they had planned for Layla. This party had been in the works for weeks, and he wasn't about to cancel it now that they had even more to celebrate. Their parents were already at the house, visiting with Lainy, and he was sure they'd been updated on how things had gone.

Smiling to himself, he could well imagine the welcome Layla was going to get when they got home. Not only did she single-handedly take down the bad guy today—a fact his dads would appreciate for sure—but she was also carrying their first grandchild. Hell, they already liked her, so she'd probably be handed the "Keys to the Kingdom" today. Looking at the sweet woman sitting so docile in his lap, he stroked his fingers down the side of her pale face and turned her so he could look directly into her eyes.

"As soon as you give a quick report to Dylan, I'll take you home, love." Her beautiful eyes filled with tears she tried to blink back.

"Can I go to your house instead? I mean, if it's okay. I'm not… well, I don't want to be alone just yet."

"Oh, love, that is exactly where I plan to take you. That is your home from now on, you understand that, right? We want you with us, and we sure don't want to wait for the wedding." *Never mind that wedding you think you have been planning for the past few weeks will actually take place tomorrow night. Your friends have outdone themselves with the preparations.*

Dylan's questions were short and sweet because they had everything on tape and the security footage from her office had captured everything as well. As the Sheriff, he needed to get to the hospital to check on the suspect, but he'd taken time to let Mia check on Layla. His wife had insisted she wanted to talk to her friend personally before being shooed into his truck. He promised to drop Mia off at their home so she could rescue the babysitter. Turning to Cash, he'd chuckled.

"Nate is an ornery little fellow, probably has that poor girl worn to a frazzle by now. I swear I'm going to retire before he and those Lamont triplets reach driving age."

Cash was relieved to see Layla's small smile and grateful for his friend's effort to lighten the mood. He was just getting ready to head home when his brothers rushed through the door. Collin picked her up in his arms, and Clay pressed as close as he could get without crawling into Collin's arms as well.

Clay's fingers stroked the side of her face with a tenderness reserved for someone cherished. "Oh, baby, you were amazing. Holy fucking hell, I was so scared and proud, all at the same time. Somebody remind me to kiss my mama's feet when we get home because now I know how scared she had to be when I started riding bulls—and they didn't have guns."

Cash heard the giggle that erupted from Layla, and it was pure music to his ears. God, he loved Clay's playful nature with her. When their mom had likened Clay to Dad Julian, she'd certainly been right. Over the years, he'd seen the youngest of his dads elicit the same reaction from his mom more times than he could count. Even though none of them ever cared which dad was their genetic father, the connection and similarities between Clay and Julian had always been the clearest.

Collin seemed nearly overcome with emotion as he nuzzled her ear and just kept tightening his hold on her. "Sweetness, I never want to be that frightened again. You inspire me, but I swear I'm starting a tab and after our sweet baby is born, you're getting every swat you earned today for pushing that asshole the way you did."

Collin's words echoed Cash's own feelings, and he knew she'd earn plenty more by the time the baby was born. He'd heard Alex and Zach say Katarina still wasn't caught up, and their children were quickly closing in on their first birthday.

He'd learned a lot from his friends who had recently become parents, but he knew Collin had already ordered a box full of books from Amazon. This would likely be like most other things; he and Clay would let Collin read up, then they'd get a report—hopefully, greatly abbreviated. Cash knew his mom and Lainy would also be a great help. Maybe if Lainy eventually found a place of her own, his parents would consider spending their summers here.

Looking over at his brothers, he was suddenly overwhelmed by the magnitude of what their sweet woman had done today. She'd faced down her worst nightmare and barely blinked. He knew it would catch up with her eventually, but the three of them would be there to catch her when she fell.

LAYLA SPENT THE next day at Rissa's spa inside The ShadowDance Club with Kat and Tori. She tried to talk Lainy and Cora into joining them, but her future in-laws insisted they each had errands to run. It seemed odd to her since Cora didn't actually live in Climax any longer, but who was she to question the sweet woman who would be her mother-in-law in a few weeks. Lying back on the softly padded lounge chair, watching Tori get her massage, Layla smiled.

"Tell us about your romantic dinner with Trace. How did he take the baby news?"

Tori's head came up, and a huge smile lit up her entire face before Rissa pushed her head back into the hole in the massage table.

"Tori, leave your head down, that isn't good for your

back and trust me when I tell you, in a couple of months, you'll be glad you listened to my warning." Rissa smiled at Layla. "Besides, as excited as you looked, I'm sure we're going to be able to hear you just fine... now spill."

"Oh, it was so perfect... well, as perfect as anything can be when it involves me serving food." Layla and Rissa both laughed because Tori's cooking disasters were nearly an urban legend. Layla knew for a fact the local fire station in Houston near Tori's apartment had offered her a standing invitation to dinner so she wouldn't cook, therefore saving them what had become a nightly run to her home.

"I had the candles lit, and Selita made the food. She told me she'd heard about my fire job in Houston. I'm not sure if she meant the time I set off those fireworks in my kitchen or the dinners at the firehouse... but anyway, she'd made this spectacular meal and even delivered it and put it in the oven and everything. Well, Trace got tied up with calves or something and didn't get home until late. Well, I'm really proud of myself for remembering to blow out the candles... but I forgot to turn down the oven." Layla started to giggle because she could already imagine how this was going to end.

"Well, you guys know how it is... I've been so damned sleepy, and I had been too excited to take a nap that afternoon, so I decided to get all dressed up and kick back in the recliner for a few minutes. I woke up, and the fracking smoke alarms were blaring like some kind of damned trumpet heralding the entrance of a king. Sure enough, Trace walked in while I was still opening windows. The house phone was ringing, and both of our cell phones were jangling as well. Before we'd gotten the first of the calls taken care of, there were two fire trucks in the yard. Oh yeah, just another episode of the *Tori's Cooking*

Comedy Show."

By this time Layla was holding her stomach because she was laughing so hard, and Rissa had given up on the massage, wrapped a sheet around Tori, and helped her sit up.

"Sorry, I promise to start over, but this is just too good to not witness face to face. Damn, I've missed hanging out with my friends."

Tori gave her a small sardonic smile. "Well, I haven't done this in a while, so you haven't missed that much from me. I'm sure you have already heard about Annie Oakley over there." Her teasing words were followed by a nod to Layla.

"Hey, let's get back to the story about you. I know you too well, I'm sure there's more." Layla was trying to act offended, but it was obvious by Tori's giggle, she hadn't taken the words seriously.

"Yes indeed, you know me too well. Okay, anyway, I'm standing out in the yard with Trace while the firefighters make sure the smoldering remains of Selita's wonderful dinner are *properly disposed of.*" She made air quotes with her last words and rolled her eyes. "Personally, I thought the hazmat suits were a tad over the top, I think the Chief was just being dramatic. But, anyway, here comes the frisky old fart with a fancy picnic basket filled with the most wonderful dinner you can ever imagine. He said Selita had told him she was cooking for me and putting it in the oven, so he had his wife make a backup dinner, just in case." She stopped talking, and all three of them had big tears streaming down their cheeks now.

"Isn't that just the sweetest thing you ever heard?" Tori sighed and then wiped away her tears before finishing her story. "Anyway, the house cleared of smoke quickly, and I don't even think we'll have to repaint the kitchen this time." Layla shook her head and laughed thinking how many layers of paint would be on those kitchen walls in the next few years.

"Well, by the time all this had happened, I was worried my news was going to be anticlimactic, you know? We were sitting in front of the fireplace later, and Trace looked over at me and asked what the white blobs had been on the kitchen table. That was all it took. I finally let the tears go, and it was as if someone had opened the floodgates of Lake Powell. Geez, pregnancy hormones are some powerful stuff, I tell ya." Layla and Rissa were back to giggling again, and Layla was glad the conversation had turned back to entertaining.

"Anyway, by the time I got to the big announcement, Trace was so stunned at my outburst, that he nearly missed it... but he is really over the moon. I'm going to have to battle him for the next seven months to do anything, I can see that now. He's already gotten all the books from your husbands," she nodded toward Rissa. "You know if you were any kind of friend at all, you'd have burned them."

"Oh no, sweet sister," Rissa shook her head. "You'll do your time just like Kat, Jenna, and I did ours. Good God, there is no one as annoying as a Dom father-to-be armed with *What to Expect When You're Expecting*, I'm here to tell you." Looking at Layla, she shook her head. "And you have three men? Oh Lord love a leper, you are really in for it." Then she burst into giggles.

"Yeah, don't I know it. Collin has already ordered a stack of books, Clay has been online reading, and Cash brought his mom and dads here. Thank God his mom is a sweetheart and a voice of reason." Layla couldn't help smiling when she thought about how loved her child was going to be and how fun it was going to be sharing this experience with Tori.

Suddenly, Tori turned to Rissa. "So how long until this hormone thing levels off? I mean, I can't track anything, and in my line of work, that's kind of essential." Tori was the only attorney in Climax after taking over the practice of the town's very happily retired former lawyer. Layla knew Tori's practice was growing by leaps and bounds, and her sweetheart of a spouse was already encouraging her to recruit a partner.

Rissa looked shocked. "Oh, I don't have a clue. I know I still feel unbalanced sometimes, and Betsy is four months old already. Kat has really struggled with postpartum depression. I know Alex and Zach finally insisted she get the medical help she'd been too stubborn to accept until recently. I've learned a lot about that from listening to them worry about her. Then there is Jenna who seems to have bounced back already… *bitch*." They all laughed because everyone who knew Jenna Lamont-Matthews loved her. She was as genuine and sincere as anyone Layla had ever met.

"When is she going to start teaching self-defense classes again? I've heard they were great, and I think they'd be a fun way to stay in shape, or at least maybe, it would be enough that I won't look like a Weeble by the time I'm six months along. Damn, I have already started outgrowing my clothes." Layla sighed, then glared at her friends when they laughed at her.

Rissa made a motion to the camera in the corner of the room. "Careful… remember this place is wired, and the guys in the Crow's Nest are the worst snitches on the planet. If they caught that 'diss,' they'll rat you out to your guys in a New York minute."

"Yippee fucking-skippy." Layla rolled her eyes. "That's all I need... hell, they've already started a Punishments Pending list. I told them they were going to need at least a ream or two of paper. Clay offered to get one of those leftover rolls of newsprint from the Gazette... the smart ass." She grinned and shook her head, thinking about how easily he could make her smile. "Oh, well. Hey, are you guys coming to Red Clouds tonight? I'm looking forward to a fun night." Both of her friends nodded, saying they were looking forward to a night out too.

"We're bringing Betsy to the Lamonts', so their nannies can watch her too. With those three, little Daniel, and Betsy, those girls are going to be busy tonight. They are both so amazing, and I think they enjoy getting to work together occasionally. Kat said Daniel and Catherine are still here, so they'll be able to help out as well. They make me wish I had parents like them."

Both women agreed, then let the conversation lull as they were each lost in their own thoughts. A couple of hours later, Clay picked her up in front of The Club, and as they made their way down the mountain, she couldn't help but notice his cat-that-swallowed-the-canary smile.

"What's with the smirk, lover?" She'd no sooner gotten the words from her mouth than he pulled off the road and headed toward a small lake at the edge of town. She'd learned there were times to ask and times to just sit back and enjoy the ride, and from the smile spreading across his face, she was guessing this little side trip was going to be a fun ride.

Chapter 25

C ASH WAS SITTING at the kitchen table late that afternoon, watching as his mom and sister teased Layla about the lack of cooking supplies in the items she'd moved into their home. She was absolutely glowing in their attention. It was obvious how much she enjoyed the banter, and he was thrilled she was able to give as good as she got.

"I'm not Betty Crocker, that's true. All the women in my family are awesome cooks, but at all of our family functions, I was more of the official photographer and chief jokester." He was surprised when she suddenly turned to him and asked, "Do you have a pair of pliers I can borrow?"

He was sure his face must have shown how surprised he was by her strange request. When he looked up, he noticed his mother standing behind Layla shaking her head back and forth and grinning.

"Love, we do indeed have pliers, and you know everything we own we will happily share with you, but would you mind telling me exactly what you plan to do with them?" She was suddenly very interested in the dish towel she had in her hands, and he wasn't sure she was going to answer at first.

"Well, shoot... this is sort of embarrassing. Can't you just let me use them for a few minutes? I promise I'm not doing anything illegal or destructive."

Now she had his full attention. What the hell was she up to? When she finally looked up, he saw what looked like embarrassment and guilt—two emotions he never wanted to see in her beautiful green eyes.

"Come here, love." He held out his hand to her and was pleased to see her tiny bare feet respond to the command in his voice almost before her mind had a chance to process the words. He pulled her onto his lap and turned her, so she was facing his brothers as well. "Tell us what this is about." His mom and Lainy slipped quietly from the room, and he was grateful for their consideration. Her smile wavered, and he saw her eyes fill with tears.

"I think I can get my favorite jeans zipped if I lie on the bed and use the pliers... and I really wanted to look hot tonight for our night out... and, well... my tummy is getting huge already."

There was a part of him that wanted to paddle her sweet ass for even thinking about using pliers to pull up the zipper on pants that were obviously going to be not only ungodly uncomfortable, but not good for her or their sweet babe. But another part of him wanted to hold her close and let her know just how thrilled they were with that tummy bump they'd all already noticed.

"Love, I can assure you I speak for all of us when I say as far as we are concerned, the larger that tummy bump gets, the happier we'll be because it will mean our child is growing healthy and strong inside his or her sweet mama. Now, if we catch wind of you trying to fit into clothes that are too tight for either you or the baby's comfort or good health, you're going to get a paddling, understood?" She nodded shyly, and he continued. "Now, Mom and Lainy helped us buy you a few new things because we knew you hadn't had time to go shopping, and we wanted you to have something special to wear tonight. Your new things are laid out on the bed upstairs. I have to head on over to Red Clouds, there are some last-minute things I want to do, so I have extra time with you tonight. Since you and Clay took a little detour this afternoon, Collin is going to help you get ready for tonight." Collin was the best choice for dressing her, anyway because his taste in clothes had always left both Cash and Clay in the dust—usually literally.

Leaning forward, Cash gave her a blistering kiss before setting her on her feet. He turned her toward Collin who pulled her close and raised her shirt to kiss her tummy.

"Sweet baby is growing, and that makes these daddies mighty happy, pet. Now, let's go upstairs and take a nice long shower. I want to lavish some attention on the two most important people in the world before we leave for the party. I'm looking forward to tonight as well, and I promise you're going to love the outfit we got for you."

Cash and Clay watched Collin lead Layla up the wide staircase and Clay grinned. "God, I love her. She's funny and smart... well, except for that pliers thing. Wonder how mom knew about that? Anyway, I'll be ready to go in just a few minutes. I can't wait to see the decorations."

As they drove the short distance to the dance club, Clay laughed as he told Cash about how easily Layla had played into his hands to stall her on the trip home from the spa. He'd spread a blanket on the sandy beach the locals had put at one end of the lake, and within minutes, she'd been fast asleep.

Walking into their new bar and dancehall, Cash was overwhelmed by the transformation. Their friends had been hard at work, but it was the small raised platform along the back wall that drew his attention. It was round, and the decorations surrounding it reflected the distinct geometric symmetry so honored by his ancestors.

The color scheme was all traditional bold colors, reflecting the natural hues that could be derived from nearby flora. They had all been thrilled when Tori told them Layla's favorite colors were those same bold colors, so he knew she was going to be thrilled with her friend's hard work.

Making sure all the final arrangements were taken care of, they were just finishing up when he looked up to see his grandmother come through the front door. He laughed when he saw her smiling and joking with Drake and Jesse. Both men dwarfed her, but she looked like she was holding her own with their teasing.

Drake Foster had been an Army Ranger before becoming a Green Beret, and despite looking like he was in his early twenties, he was actually thirty-four. Drake's sandy blonde hair always looked like it needed to be cut and the women who frequented the club had nicknamed him Surfer the first night they'd opened.

They'd all laughed that night as they sat at a back table with the Lamonts, watching the women flock around Drake like bees to honey. Zach had laughed when he'd speculated aloud, "Wonder what those women would say if they knew about his whip fetish or that he knows about a hundred ways to kill a man with his bare hands?"

Alex had shaken his head. "Well, several of those young ladies wouldn't have any reservations about the whip, as a matter of fact, he might not ever be able to get rid of them." He laughed to himself before turning to Cash. "When we recruited him, he told us he hadn't killed anyone in his last six months in the Green Berets. When I checked, I learned he'd been on accumulated leave and home in San Diego for five of those months." They had all laughed because they appreciated the man's humor. "I'm glad he's working here between assignments for us. He needs to be busy, and I know he and Jesse are hoping to find a woman to share. They were at our home a few weeks ago, and they're both great with kids, so I hope it works out for them soon."

Cash had known Jesse Hunt forever. The man was a genius according to Collin, and that was quite a recommendation coming from the man who'd maxed out every test the school had ever tried to give him. Jesse moved to Houston and went to work for Collin right out of high school and from all appearances, hadn't spent much of the money he'd earned, so Cash was sure he wasn't working because he needed the money.

Standing six and a half feet tall, Jesse was imposing but not overwhelming because of his slender frame. Cash knew Jesse was also a childhood friend of Noah Drummond, so he'd considered asking the man about the history between Noah and Lainy. He probably would, but not tonight— tonight he intended to get married, have their commitment ceremony, then go home and make love to his wife after they'd enjoyed their party for a while.

Making his way over to his grandmother he warmed at the smile she gave him. "Shimá sání Níyol, I am so happy you are here." Using the Navajo word for grandmother was always his initial greeting for her because he knew how much she appreciated him honoring their heritage.

He had always been her favored grandchild, there was no use denying what was obvious, but Níyol Red Cloud held a very special place in his heart as well. As a child, he had teased her about her name being the Navajo word for wind, always telling her to stop blowing smoke at him. Her response had always been she was named after the spirit-wind that spoke to her. As he'd grown up, he'd understood just how impressive her gift was—her conversations with the spirit wind was a gift to everyone who knew her. Her ability to understand the soul of another and to foresee the future was almost frightening. Damn, thinking about her teaming up with Mitch Grayson was scary as hell.

As he wrapped the tiny woman in his arms, she placed her hands on either side of his face and pulled him down, looking at him so intently, he was sure she was looking into the deepest recesses of his soul.

"He's going to look just like you. I'll come and give him a blessing and weave a protection for him. But tonight... oh, tonight is for wrapping his sweet mama in the love of my three grandsons."

Cash wasn't at all surprised she'd known Layla was pregnant. Most grandmothers would have been, at the very least, suspicious of the rushed plans. Cash also knew she wouldn't judge, and heaven knew, she was no one's fool. But the fact that she'd just told him he was the baby's genetic father and his son would look like him pleased him more than he knew it should.

"Thank you, but we might want to keep some of that information to ourselves at least for a bit. His sweet mama is still trying to get used to the idea he's on his way." He saw her grin and knew she understood.

"I am so happy you boys found her. She needed you just as much as you needed her." He used his thumbs to wipe away the tears that were spilling over to trail down her sun-weathered cheeks. "I plan to be around for a while, your other babies will need me as well, but first I have to help your sister." Grabbing his large hand in her small ones, she smiled.

"She is going to be a challenge, I know, she holds tightly to a hurt that never really was." He noticed her grip was still firm even though her hands felt smaller than he remembered. "She's going to learn the truth soon. I hope she can accept the truth both within and around her." Cash found himself chuckling along with her because they both knew what a challenge it was for Ilaina Red Cloud to admit being wrong.

Cash led her to one of the front tables and seated her. She would be sitting with his parents front and center—in the place of honor they all deserved. Looking up, he saw the front doors open and smiled as friends and family began filling the room. He could hardly wait for Collin to arrive with Layla. He knew his brother would enjoy dressing her up for the evening. Collin had never had any trouble enjoying the perks of his wealth when it came to clothing. Collin's fashion tastes had always been more in line with Lainy's. The two of them often teased Cash and Clay about being adopted.

Cash wasn't that surprised when Clay walked up and asked him for the third time if he had the ring. Pulling the small velvet box from his pocket, he flipped the lid open so his youngest brother could see for himself Cash did indeed have it. When he showed it to his mom and Lainy, he was pleased to hear them gasp.

Their friend, Evan Taylor had designed and made the ring with their input. The band was made up of three small bands with one very large diamond flanked by two slightly smaller stones. Evan, who was a fellow Dom and member of The ShadowDance Club, had been happy to rush their order when they'd explained the surprise they were planning for Layla.

The gold band had been Cash's choice because he wanted her to know his love was pure, and she'd always be his most treasured gift. Collin had chosen a platinum band because he was the strictest Dom and wanted her to understand his strength would always be for her alone. Clay had smiled and said he wanted white gold for his band because he wanted to be her knight in shining armor and the one who could bring sunshine into her darkest days.

Feeling his phone vibrate in his pocket, he pulled it out and smiled as he announced, "They're on their way." He saw Clay's face light up in anticipation as they both headed to the door. Cash wasn't sure he'd ever been this nervous. He'd been in some of the most dangerous places on earth and dealt with evil few people ever face and never blinked. It was an amusing irony his palms were sweating over one tiny blonde bombshell.

Cash and Clay were just walking up to the entrance when Collin escorted Layla through the double doors. She didn't seem to notice the quieter music or the decorations. Instead, she ran up and threw her arms out to the side and spun around.

"Look at me! This dress is so amazing. I feel like a princess. Thank you so much and check these out." Pointing out her sexy sandals, Cash grinned because Collin had obviously carried her over the gravel parking lot because there wasn't any evidence of mud on her dainty pink-tipped toes. "I got a lift from a very handsome gentleman, or I'd have gotten them dirty." She grinned and leaned over and kissed Collin when he finally caught up with her.

Cash couldn't help but laugh. She was so thrilled with the clothes they'd gotten her, she still hadn't taken time to look around. Having a woman who could find such joy in a simple gift was rare indeed. He'd been with women over the years who were so busy "playing to an audience," they were never fully focused on him, so her ability to turn out everything but him was seductive in itself. He'd talked with both of his brothers and hadn't been surprised when they had both made the same observation.

"Love, you look amazing, just as we knew you would." And Cash meant each word. The dress they'd chosen was what his sister called eucalyptus. When Clay had called it green, Lainy had patiently corrected him—twice. His fashion savvy sister had insisted the color would be perfect to bring out the unique greens and hidden blues of Layla's eyes, and as usual, she'd been right. The fit of the dress hid the slight bump they'd all noticed around her waistline, and the fabric floated around her in shimmering, soft waves.

He knew the minute she noticed things weren't as they usually were; he saw her eyes track behind him, then dart from him to Clay, then to Collin before returning to him.

"What's going on?" The slight trembling in her voice wasn't lost on him, and he pulled her into his embrace. When he finally released her into Clay's arms, he watched as Clay turned her, so her back was flush against his chest.

Cash was sure she hadn't noticed they'd been leading her slowly to the edge of the dance floor. He watched as her eyes quickly sweep the room before locking on the stage for a few seconds and returning to him. God, he loved the way she looked to him for guidance.

"Smile, love because I promise you there are lots of cameras pointed our way right now, and I'd like our children to look back on these pictures and see how happy their sweet mama was when her men threw her a surprise wedding.

"A surprise *wedding*? Seriously?" He almost panicked when her voice was little more than a squeak, but then the smile that lit up her face looked like it was reflecting every star in the sky. "Oh my God, that is the most romantic thing I've ever heard." She stepped away from Clay and turned, so she was facing all three of them. "You are the most wonderful men, and I'm so very lucky." After a few seconds of uncomfortable silence, she leaned close and spoke softly, so only those really close by could hear, "What are we waiting for?"

Cash laughed out loud and scooped her up into his arms, making his way to the stage. The local Justice of the Peace made quick work of the official ceremony, but it was the Commitment Ceremony that sealed their hearts together for eternity. As the spiritual leader of their family, their grandmother spoke the blessing over each of them as they pledged their love to one another.

Even though he was her official husband, none of them would ever recognize any difference in their relationships. Each of them would be just as committed and *married* as the others. When they had finalized their vows, they were swarmed by family and friends as congratulations, and well wishes surrounded them. He watched his sweet grandmother raise her weathered fingers to gently wipe the tears from Layla's cheeks and thought his heart would burst with joy.

Cash extended his hand to her, and his entire world narrowed to the two of them as she placed her hand in his without hesitation. Leading her on to the dance floor, he whispered, "Let's get this party started. Our friends are waiting for our first dance so they can join us." He moved her skillfully around the floor as "Lost in This Moment" by Big and Rich played. He and his brothers had each chosen a song that spoke to them. Cash let the words speak for him until the dance was nearly done.

"You remind me there is goodness and joy in this crazy world. I spent so many years seeing only the worst of humanity, I worried my soul wouldn't be able to overcome the darkness. Then I found you, and it was as if my spirit had been thrown a lifeline. Thank you, love."

Turning her into Clay's embrace, Cash smiled when he heard the first strains of "I Cross My Heart" by George Strait. Walking to the edge of the dance floor, he laughed when Collin asked him, "Remember when he was in school and drove us all nuts replaying that movie over and over? Damn, what was the name of that? Oh, yea, *Pure Country*. Christ, how could I have forgotten?"

"Bet Mom could have told you in her sleep. I'll never forget her taking that disc out of the player and breaking it apart, then pouring charcoal lighter over the small pile and torching them in the middle of the driveway. Damn, the look on Clay's face was priceless. I don't think I have laughed that hard since—well, ever. The dads decided she was skating close to the edge and took her on that nice cruise. I've often figured she was smarter than we all gave her credit because she'd been trying to get them to go on that vacation for a long time. Hell, knowing her and Clay, it may well have all been staged." They both grinned as Clay danced Layla around the floor and ended right in front of them before twirling her directly into Collin's waiting embrace.

WHEN THE FIRST strains of "I Don't Want to Miss a Thing" by Aerosmith filled the room, there was a collective female sigh heard throughout the room. Collin looked down into Layla's beautiful green eyes and smiled.

"Did you hear that, sweetheart? Every woman in the

room knows exactly how much I love you because I have chosen this song for our first dance as husband and wife." When she seemed frozen in place, he shook his head and grinned. She'd already danced with his brothers, but he suspected she'd just realized all eyes were focused on her. Leaning forward, he kissed her on the forehead. "Dancing is just a conversation between souls—talk to me."

She fit perfectly in his arms, and they glided over the floor as if they were one person. He'd considered making the moment a bit more erotic, but he hadn't wanted her to have any reason to feel embarrassment during this party. So, he was forced to keep all those thoughts to himself, for the time being.

They were leaving on a short trip first thing tomorrow morning. Neither Collin nor his brothers had wanted to have to travel tonight because they had wanted Layla to be able to enjoy the party, and from the looks on her friends' faces, they intended to grab her for one of their girls' dances as soon as his time with her was through.

"Collin." His name on her sweet lips brought him back from his musings. "I just wanted you to know I love you very much. I love all three of you with all of my heart." She almost stumbled as her eyes filled with tears, but he helped her get back in step quickly. "I don't know that I've told you how scared I'd always been that when my uncle got out of prison someday, he would kill me, but you and Cash and Clay... well, your love made me brave, and that's the very best kind of love there is."

This time it was Collin who nearly stumbled. "You take my breath away, sweetheart, and you are right.

Love that strengthens you is the best love of all."

Books by Avery Gale

The ShadowDance Club
Katarina's Return – Book One
Jenna's Submission – Book Two
Rissa's Recovery – Book Three
Trace & Tori – Book Four
Reborn as Bree – Book Five
Red Clouds Dancing – Book Six
Perfect Picture – Book Seven

Club Isola
Capturing Callie – Book One
Healing Holly – Book Two
Claiming Abby – Book Three

Masters of the Prairie Winds Club
Out of the Storm
Saving Grace
Jen's Journey
Bound Treasure
Punishing for Pleasure
Accidental Trifecta
Missionary Position
Another Second Chance
Star-Crossed Miracles
Dusted Star
Lilly's Choice

The Wolf Pack Series
Mated – Book One
Fated Magic – Book Two
Tempted by Darkness – Book Three

The Knights of the Boardroom
Book One
Book Two
Book Three

The Morgan Brothers of Montana
Coral Hearts – Book One
Dancing with Deception – Book Two
Caged Songbird – Book Three
Game On – Book Four
Well Bred – Book Five

Mountain Mastery
Well Written
Savannah's Sentinel
Sheltering Reagan

Enchanted Holidays
The Christmas Painting

I would love to hear from you!

Website:
www.averygale.com

Facebook:
facebook.com/avery.gale.3

Twitter:
@avery_gale